Scotsman

Jolene Bride

Contents

A Proper Murder...

1 8 December 1813, Durham, England

It's not every day that a young lady of good social standing finds a dead body.

Lottie chewed on her thumbnail as she walked along the beach, her mind racing. She recalled the altercation she had had with Mr. Farraday the night before and the way he had threatened her. How did he know? Did he actually have any evidence?

"I protected myself. How could that be so wrong? Why must I pay for the selfishness of a man who caused his own doom?" Lottie muttered. In her other hand, she clutched her little notebook of inventions so hard that the leather binding creaked. Only the night before, she had held a knife in that shaky hand, pointing it at Mr. Farraday. "There has to be a way to stop him—"

Her toe collided with something firm and she tripped forward onto the wet sand.

"Blast these skirts!" she spat out a mouthful of gritty sand and laughed ruefully at herself. Her adopted mother, the Countess of Durham, would likely faint at her foul language.

Lottie rolled over and sat up to brush off the fine blue linen of her skirts. They were already muddy and wet from the hour's walk from Lampton Castle, traipsing through the freshly fallen snow.

Then she spotted what had tripped her. Or rather, who had tripped her.

"M-mr. Farraday?" Lottie asked, touching his shoulder. "Are you alright.. .?" He was awfully pale, and his clothes were soaked, the rising tide lapping at the shredded remains of his grey coat fanned out around him on the sand. A dark red splotch stained his chest around a long, narrow cut.

Dread pooled in her gut and she scrambled backward with a scream. "Help! Somebody, help!"

But she was alone on the beach, and as her shock at the sight of a dead body drained away, a new thought made her stop shouting for help.

Someone had killed Mr. Farraday before she could.

But did that mean her secret had gone with him to the grave?

***Two days earlier...

Lottie Atwell had two dreams in life: establish herself as an inventor and obtain a love-filled marriage. Since there were few men who could tolerate the former, she had resigned herself to give up on the latter.

Of course, there were other reasons she had given up any hope of finding a doting husband. Being betrayed by the man she fancied herself in love with and being kidnapped by the French—twice— had entirely soured her opinion of men.

Lottie carefully sidestepped the over-eager hands of her dance partner and forced a genteel smile. "Thank you, sir, but I confess that I am quite tired from the last two reels." The country ball hosted by one of the local gentlemen of Durham, a Mr. Brighton, was quite different from the balls in London and Bath that she had attended. The men were much more careless with their manners here and tended to hold onto the ladies a little longer than necessary.

Her younger self would have enjoyed the doting attention of the handsome men who flocked to her pretty looks—and her large dowery—but Lottie wasn't a little girl anymore. She had learned the hard way that the world was not to be trusted.

Although she had been raised in America, the declaration of war between Britain and America in 1812 had forced her older sister, Fidelia, to accept the help of the British Lord William Greyville to escape a French captain who had developed an obsession with Lottie.

Now, a year later, Lottie found herself trying to play the part of a ditzy debutante at ton events, the adopted daughter of the Earl and Countess of Durham.

"But I've only just begun to tell you about my prized hunting hound—" the young man with a weak jaw and pouchy belly insisted, oblivious to her protests.

"A tale I'm sure Miss Lottie would find absolutely fascinating," a new voice interrupted.

Lottie looked up to see a scarecrow of a man towering next to her, his sunken eyes and cheeks hauntingly dark in the dim light of the dancehall.

"Unfortunately, I have claimed this next set. Miss Lottie?" he held out his hand.

The thought of touching him made her shiver. "We haven't been properly introduced, sir," she said, lifting her chin in a poor imitation of her sister's bravado.

"Ah, but we have, don't you remember? Mr. Brighton introduced us at the beginning of the ball," the scarecrow-man said, his uncommonly smooth voice at odds with his severe appearance.

Lottie blinked, trying to remember. "Oh... yes. Mr...?"

"Jonathan Farraday," he said with a deep bow. He took her hand without her consent and pulled her in line for another set. Thankfully, this one was much slower.

Lottie looked around for her older sister, Fidelia, and brother-in-law William, praying they would notice her discomfort. She spied Fidelia's bright red hair in the corner of the room, dancing playfully around her husband, who shuffled awkwardly with his heavy cane. He'd been shot in the leg when trying to rescue his wife from a kidnapping attempt the year before.

Fidelia and William, who were always very attentive to Lottie, were finally enjoying themselves, and Lottie didn't want to disturb them. She wished she could have refused, but it was horribly impolite to decline an invitation, as the Countess had so often drilled into Lottie's head. Instead, she forced another smile and determined to play the part of a brainless debutante, at least for one more dance.

"Have you ever been to Scotland, Miss Lottie?" Mr. Farraday asked as they rounded their neighbors in the slow movements of the dance.

"No, sir, I have not," she said pleasantly through gritted teeth.

"Hmm, you really must go some day. I just returned from a delightful house party where I heard the juiciest bit of gossip. Wouldn't you like to hear it?" he peered down at her with a greasy leer.

"Gossip-mongering is more the realm of my friend Miss Palmer," Lottie said and fixed her eyes on the sides of the room and the other dancers, anywhere to avoid looking at that predatory smile again.

"Ah, yes. The ton can be so very vicious. A lady's reputation is so delicate, wouldn't you say? Even being alone with a man at, say... an abandoned mill, could ruin a young lady and her family forever." His voice was casual, but it sent shards of ice into Lottie's lower back.

She froze. The neighboring dancers continued to move around her, and but suddenly flashes of moonlight through the walls of an abandoned mill flitted through her mind. The wings of birds fluttered frantically in the rafters of the mill, startled from her pounding footsteps.

Mr. Farraday clucked his tongue, false concern oozing from his tone and expression as he placed a hand under her arm. "Come, Miss Lottie, you look rather faint. A breath of fresh air would do you good," he said, and pulled her through the crowd.

Lottie pulled at her hand weakly, but the memories of the darkened mill kept her captive away. The music soured and screeched in her ears.

***

The punch landed hard on Thomas Hawthorne's cheek, catching him by surprise. He stumbled backward and collided with a tree in the garden. The glowing lights from the country ball inside Brighton Manor illuminated the skeletal remains of the garden, casting eerie shadows on the churned-up snow.

He grunted, touching the spot. It would hardly bruise. He scoffed. "Still punch like a girl, eh Lord Campbell?"

Lord Campbell smoothed his red-brown hair and straightened his lapels. "Gentlemen such as I do not tussle with society's scum," he spat. "I'll save my strength for more worthy opponents."

Thomas leaned his tall, broad frame against the tree and nodded with a sardonic laugh. "Aye, m'Lord."

"Perhaps that will make you think twice before you challenge my honor again," Lord Campbell turned to go back inside Brighton Manor. Thomas had sent him a note through a servant, calling him outside for a confrontation.

Thomas just hadn't expected it to become physical so quickly.

"Honor?" Thomas spat. "The only honor ye possess is what ye've stolen from the many young ladies ye've tricked and taken advantage of. How long will ye continue down this path? The rumors about ye being a rake will bring scandal upon yer family. Think about yer sister, if nothing else!"

Lord Campbell turned back and glared down his nose at Thomas. "I will not be chastised by a stable boy. If you are so worried about Catriona, go see her yourself," he gestured to the ball with a mock bow. "I have brought her to Lord Greyville's house party to secure her a marriage, if you must know."

Thomas paused, his hand balling into a fist at the mention of Catriona's name. She had only been a girl when he'd last seen her, just a child. Lord Campbell was already trying to marry her off? Most likely to bring himself some advantage with no thought to his sister's feelings, no doubt.

He should have beaten Lord Campbell to a pulp when he had the chance.

"No? Oh, I forgot," Lord Campbell sneered. "You are just a mangy mutt that ran away from the war with his tail between his legs when he got scared."

The words were a slap across the face. "I'm warning ye, Campbell," he growled, "stop yer games before Catriona gets hurt."

Lord Campbell's eyes narrowed, and his lips twitched. "I think we both know who hurt her more. For someone who talks so much about honor, you abandoned Catriona rather quickly, wouldn't you say?"

Silently, Thomas watched Lord Campbell smooth his hair once again and return to the ball.

Thomas touched the tender spot on his cheek and frowned. Had Lord Campbell mentioned Lord Greyville? Did that mean—

Movement from the corner of his eye drew his attention. He ducked behind the tree, careful not to be seen, and watched as a tall, lanky man led a young woman out of the ball and into the garden. She seemed in a daze, her bright blond hair shining like a beacon in the wintry moonlight.

Thomas caught his breath, a familiar ache starting in his chest. He only felt that when he thought of— "Lottie Atwell."

***

Lottie blinked, finally pushing away the nightmares she had tried so hard to forget for the last 11 months. How had they suddenly arrived out into the garden?

"You seemed quite shocked to hear such a rumor," Mr. Farraday said with mock concern. "Do you happen to know the young lady in question?"

"I d-don't know what you're talking about," she said even as her voice cracked. Only three people knew about that night: Lottie's sister Fidelia, her husband William, and Thomas, the boy who had defended Lottie's honor. They were the only ones still living, that is.

Mr. Farraday clutched her arm and dragged her close, his hot breath burning her neck as he leaned down to hiss in her ear. "If you can imagine what the ton would say about such a scandalous rumor, what would they say if they knew you had killed a man?"

***Hi friends!

Thank you for your patience and support while waiting for this book!

What do you think of the first chapter? What things are you hoping to see from this story? I'd love to hear from you in the comments below!! Your input made the first book in the series so much better and I'd love to get your help with this one, too!

A Handsome Rescuer

F ear burned within Lottie, a blinding terror that she hadn't felt since the night she had killed Monsieur Le Coquin. "Let go of me," she cried, prying at the fingers that clutched her arm tightly.

"Not until you agree to my demand, Miss Lottie. That is how black-mail works, you see—" Mr. Farraday's calm words were cut off sharply as someone grabbed him by the collar from behind. He gurgled as the hand tightened, causing his cravat to cut against his throat.

"The wee lass said to let go," a deep voice said and the man, hidden from Lottie's view by Mr. Farraday's head, wrenched Mr. Farraday away from Lottie, tossing him like a ragdoll against the bushes.

Lottie looked up at her rescuer as he stepped into the moonlight. She would recognize those gentle brown eyes and tousled black hair anywhere. "T-Thomas?"

The young man who towered over her smiled in a shy, crooked way. "Aye, Miss Lottie."

Her relief made her forget any sense of propriety and she lurched for-ward, wrapping her arms around his waist as her knees buckled. Thomas

Hawthorne. Her rescuer. The man who had defended her and helped her kill Monsieur Le Coquin that night in the old mill. The only man—other than her brother-in-law—that she could trust.

Thomas had been a stranger then, just a passerby who heard her screams and came to her aid just in time. Thomas had held Le Coquin back long enough for Lottie to wrap an old pulley system's rope around her attacker and hoist him over a hole in the floor. The rigging had been too old, however, and the ropes snapped. Some might have said that it was an accident that Le Coquin fell four stories to his death. But Lottie had known the ropes would break. She had known exactly what would happen to the man who had tormented her for the last two years.

Awkwardly, Thomas patted Lottie on the back in return with one of his large hands as if afraid he might break her. Keeping one arm around her shoulders, he turned to look at Mr. Farraday, who had just managed to detangle himself from the brambles.

"Ah, I see that scandals abound with you, Miss Lottie," Mr. Farraday scoffed, brushing dead leaves from his coat. "Caught in a compromising position with yet another man, I see."

"I'm just Lord Greyville's stable hand," Thomas said, his quiet voice rumbling in a dangerous manner. "Any servant would come to the defense of their master's charge."

Lottie looked up at him sharply. William's stable hand? Was he lying to protect her honor again?

"Now," Thomas gently pressed Lottie behind him and marched several steps forward to loom above Mr. Farraday. "What business do ye have with Miss Lottie?"

Mr. Farraday eyed Thomas for a long moment and something flickered in his eyes. Lottie would have called it recognition. "A stable hand." Mr. Farraday sucked his teeth thoughtfully. Finally, he bowed slightly to Lottie.

As he passed Thomas, he paused beside Lottie under the guise of straightening his cravat. He whispered so quietly that she doubted Thomas could hear. "I shall see you tomorrow at Lord Greyville's house party. We will finish our discussion then. And if you try to plan something, remember this: what I possess is enough to shock even the Prince Regent."

With a gleam in his eye, he continued with a confident stride back towards the ball.

This is a dream. Lottie's legs felt numb and she stumbled once he vanished from sight. A nightmare. How can he possibly know my secret?

Thomas caught her with one hand around her waist and the other at her elbow. "Miss Lottie?" he asked. "Who was that man? What does he want?"

Lottie stared blindly ahead, her mind working at a furious pace. She had to stop this. If her secret was revealed, then everything that William and Fidelia had fought for, everything Lottie had been through, it would all be for nothing. "His name is Mr. Farraday."

"Did he hurt ye?" Thomas's quiet voice calmed her racing mind as he hesitantly touched her shoulder.

Lottie shook her head. She forced a smile and stepped back to a respectable distance. She couldn't let him suspect what Mr. Farraday knew.

The truth wouldn't hurt just Lottie's reputation.

Thomas could be sentenced to death if anyone knew that he had helped her kill Le Coquin.

***

Thomas's worry only increased when Lottie forced a smile.

"It's nothing. Just another suitor with overly eager hands. Thank you for your help," she said with a confidence that he did not believe for a moment.

He opened his mouth to challenge her sudden change of mood, but she tipped her head to the side, her eyes bright. The sight left him strangely unable to breathe.

"What are you doing here? I haven't seen you since..." she paused, and her face darkened momentarily. "You left without saying goodbye that night on the beach in Budle."

Thomas dropped his gaze. After the incident in the mill, he had delivered Lottie and her sister Fidelia to Lord Greyville on the beach near the seaside town of Budle. Fidelia had offered him work in the stables, but the longer Thomas stood guard over Lottie through that night, the more he realized he couldn't stay by her.

Thomas understood that if he remained near her, he would surely lose his heart. So, he had left in the morning without a word, retreating into the world of anonymity in which he had sheltered since his return from the war.

"I... Forgive me for leaving. But I'm here now," he said with a shrug. Somehow, even being near this woman for a short amount of time made him lose any semblance of intelligence.

The punch landed on his shoulder. He looked up in surprise. For someone so small and innocent looking, she had quite the arm.

Thomas gawked at her. "Did ye just punch me?"

Lottie pressed her lips together to hide a grin. "That's for leaving without a goodbye. I saved your life, you know. According to ancient codes of warriors and clansmen, your life is bound to mine."

Slowly, he smiled. Even after receiving such a fright from Mr. Farraday, Lottie could still maintain her bright spirit. Thomas had seen that same resilience that night at the beach near Budle.

Thomas knew that Lottie was no wilting flower, no matter how young or sweet she appeared. There was a side to her like a knife's blade—wickedly sharp.

"Aye, wee lassie. I suppose my life belongs to ye," he bowed playfully. "does that mean I shall now be subject to many experiments and inventions?"

Lottie laughed and the sound made Thomas a little weak in the knees. Bright, bubbly, contagious. She was a ray of light, even in the dark, snowy evening; which is exactly why he had left that night in Budle.

Thomas allowed himself to soak in the warmth of her company for only a moment longer before he forced away the smile that tugged at his lips when he looked at her. "Miss Lottie, ye should return to the ball. I fear yer sister and brother-in-law will be worried about ye."

Lottie blinked and that hard look returned to her eye. Whatever had happened with Mr. Farraday, it had been enough to bring about the feral expression that he had seen at the mill when she had kicked the lever that sent Le Coquin to his death.

She curtsied. "You're right. I should go."

He bowed slightly, keeping his head ducked as he waited for her to leave. A small, warm hand slid into his and Thomas's chest tightened. He looked up sharply.

Lottie stepped closer, her brows pinching together as she looked up at him, holding his hand. "Will I see you again?"

Heart pounding, Thomas nodded hesitantly. "Aye. I'll... be near. My life belongs to ye, remember?"

Lottie smiled in relief. She squeezed his hand tightly for just a moment before slipping away again.

Not only my life, wee lassie. Thomas thought mournfully as he watched her leave. If I am not careful, my entire heart will belong to ye as well.

*** Lottie wrung her hands together as she stumbled back to the ball. Once she left Thomas's comforting presence, her wild fear returned. Mr. Farraday said he had proof. But what could that be? What were the demands he mentioned? What was he going to make her do?

Oh, how she wished that wretched man would just drop dead.

***Hey Guys! What do you think of Thomas? He's such a sweetie <3 And what do you think of Lottie's predicament? I'd love to hear your thoughts in the comments below!

If you liked this chapter, please vote and comment!

P.s. know any actors that would be good as Thomas? I'm looking for suggestions!!

Lottie Claims Thomas

Thomas fidgeted under Lord Greyville's piercing blue stare as they stood alone in the stables the next morning. The horses at Lambton Castle were well known throughout England for their excellent pedigrees and Thomas had to admit that the reputation was warranted.

Lord Greyville began slowly. "You want to... work. Here? In my stables?"

"After I found Miss Lottie at the mill last year, Lady Greyville offered me work. I... was detained for a time, but now I am here and humbly ask that ye uphold her offer," Thomas said, wishing for all the world he could be somewhere else. His eyes kept flitting to the castle where he knew Lottie would be.

Lord Greyville leaned heavily upon his cane and sighed. "When Fidelia told me about the young man who saved our Lottie, I never would have guessed it was you. Thomas, do you not understand who you are? Who your father is?"

"My father and I want nothing to do with each other. After I returned from the war on the continent, my father declared me dead to him. All I wish now is to survive," Thomas shrugged and patted the nose of a pretty dun-colored mare who hung her head over her stall door. "Please, Lord Greyville."

"We're childhood friends, Thomas, the least you can do is call me 'William.' We are equals after all." William frowned at his companion and Thomas shrugged sheepishly.

William continued. "But why here? Surely there are less conspicuous places to find employment. What if someone recognizes you?" William asked. A cart drawn by two large mules creaked to a halt outside the stable doors and men began to unload several boxes and a few small barrels.

Thomas moved closer to William and lowered his voice as they watched the workman. He folded his arms as he said, "Lord Campbell has brought Catriona with him to your house party to try and arrange a marriage for her."

"Ah," William nodded with understanding. "You wish to keep an eye on her."

And Lottie, Thomas added silently, but he dared not voice the feelings that were beginning to grow within him for William's sister-in-law. "Catriona was only a child when I left for war, so I do not fear that she will recognize me. The same applies to everyone else who may have the opportunity to recognize me. There's something suspicious about Lord Campbell's plan for her... I should at least try to protect her if I can. I owe her that much."

The workmen finished and set off again. William stamped his heavy cane and reached out to shake Thomas's hand. "Although I believe this is far below your station, I understand your plight. I will help you as best as I can. It's the least I can do for the friend who rescued me from more scrapes that I can count during our time at Eton. Besides, I needed a good stablemaster," he said with a wink. "It'll be fun to see you covered in horse manure."

As Thomas accepted the handshake with a laugh, a bright voice interrupted them.

"William? Have my supplies arrived? I heard Cook say that she directed the workman down here—" Lottie broke off as she rounded the stable doors and paused, her golden-blond hair pulled up into a messy bun and secured with a ragged scarf.

Thomas's breath snagged in his throat and he suddenly felt too warm for the chilly winter morning. "Hello, Miss Lottie."

"Thomas!" she grinned and ran to meet him. Thomas and William both grunted with surprise when she threw her arms around the Scotsman.

"Lottie," William muttered and poked her with his cane. "Show a little propriety, please. He is 'Mr. Hawthorne' to you."

Lottie lifted her head away from Thomas's chest and smirked at William with a teasing glint in her eye. "He's 'Thomas' to me now. He's promised to be my guinea pig for inventions. He says he belongs to me now."

Thomas sputtered and tried to pry one of his arms out of her tight hug. She had a remarkably good grip. "That's—it's not—She makes it sound a lot worse than what I said—"

William folded his arms and arched one eyebrow at Thomas. "Oh, you belong to my sister now?"

Thomas laughed nervously and finally managed to pry himself out of her arms. He held up his hands towards William; that cane looked like it could do some serious damage. "It's—really, I just said that I would—please don't kill me."

William gave Lottie a look that said 'we will discuss this later, young lady,' and gestured out the door with a sigh of long-suffering. "Please stop harassing my new stable master. Your packages are stacked outside, although I have no idea why they would deliver such dangerous items to my horses."

Lottie squealed in delight and rushed back out the door. She pried the lid off one of the wooden boxes and examined the contents, her face glowing. "Thomas, can you help me carry these up to my laboratory?" she asked as she rifled through another box.

"Good luck," William muttered and nudged Thomas closer to Lottie. "If your life belongs to her now, then you'll likely be blown up or run through with a spear in the next twenty-four hours."

Thomas's sound of surprise was cut off as Lottie ran up, grabbed his hand, and dragged him over to her packages. She had closed the boxes before he could see what was inside, but the outside was clearly labeled with the word 'danger.' William was just joking... right?

Thomas heaved the largest box onto his shoulder and Lottie led the way up to the castle and through a side door, struggling with one of the small barrels. Lambton Castle had been built in the Norman style, complete with turrets set at the corners and two rising from the center of the structure, and all of the walls were lined with parapets. The large stone blocks, originally a gold limestone, had become discolored with time, but the castle was still just as stunning as it was massive. Lottie led him to the turret rising from the center of the castle and up the tight spiral staircase.

"Why are we going up here?" Thomas paused to lean against the wall, panting under the weight of the box and the strain of carrying it up four flights of stairs.

Lottie stopped to rest as well, blowing her curly blond hair out of her eyes. "The upper level of the turret was converted into a bedroom by one of William's more eccentric ancestors. My brother-in-law grew tired of my inventions causing problems throughout the rest of the castle, so he allowed me to take over the turret and turn it into my very own laboratory."

They continued up the stairs and paused by another door.

"Is this your laboratory?" Thomas asked, grateful for the chance to catch his breath.

Lottie shook her head with a secretive glint in her eye. "It leads out to the main roof of the castle. Come on, I want to show you something." She pushed the door open and directed Thomas to leave his load to the side for a moment.

Thomas's heart lifted at the pride that glowed on her face as she led him to the middle of the castle's rampart. He had never been comfortable with heights, but he tried to ignore the way his stomach twisted as Lottie leaned over the edge of the stone wall without an ounce of fear.

"Look!" she said, pointing down the side of the castle. It was a long, four-story drop to the stones below and Thomas cringed at the sight. He followed Lottie's hand to see a makeshift pully system that hung from several ropes tied around a raised stone set in the wall. "It's a pully system. I made it so that I wouldn't have to carry things up and down the stairs. It takes about three people to operate—one to load at the bottom and pull the ropes, and two at the top to steady and unload. We can ask some of the servants to help us."

Thomas quickly straightened and kept fixed his eyes firmly on the stones below his feet. He wouldn't fall, he reassured himself. "Does the height nae bother ye, wee lassie?" he asked, swallowing hard.

Lottie cocked her head. "Why should it?"

"The pully..." Thomas gestured awkwardly to the rigging. "Does it nae bring back bad memories of—"

Lottie's face hardened and she clasped her hands together. "Scientists don't allow bad memories to get in the way of progress. The pully system is still useful to me, regardless of... of..." her voice trailed off and Thomas noticed that her knuckles were turning white.

Lottie's countenance brightened and she led him back towards the door. "Come, I want to show you my laboratory," she said cheerily, but her voice sounded brassy, like the sudden mood change was forced and unnatural.

Thomas followed along at a slower pace. Clearly, the little lady had no desire to remember what had happened that night at the mill with Monsiuer Le Coquin. Was she still tormented by it? Thomas wondered. But he knew not to pressure her. He had enough of his own demons dogging his every step. He knew the haunted look in her eyes—he had seen it reflected in the mirror often.

Thomas lifted the box back onto his shoulder and followed Lottie up the last spiral of stairs. He finally understood why she seemed to be so proud of her laboratory when she opened the door at the top. It was a large, round room with stone walls, a wooden floor, and a cozy fireplace, and every inch of it spoke of science.

Along the circular walls hung ragged tapestries, pully systems, and various instruments that Thomas could not even begin to describe. Several tables were piled with more projects, most only partially finished, and a rickety writing desk sat near the fireplace. The only light other than the glow of the fire gleamed through the two narrow Arrow Loops set high in the walls. At least glass had been placed over them to keep out the wind.

It was impressive if a bit overwhelming in its disorder.

As Thomas placed the box in the center of the room so he could turn around, he spied a floppy-eared cat curled up on a worn-out settee near the fireplace. "Who is this?" he crouched beside the cat, who stretched a dainty nose out to his hand, headbutting Thomas's knuckles.

"That's Puppy," Lottie said, scratching the creature behind his ears. "My faithful co-explorer of the sciences." The cat stood, stretched, and proceeded to zip around the room in circles like the devil was after him.

Thomas laughed. "And a jolly good day to you, too," he called after the streak of white and brown. He turned his attention to her other inventions, pausing beside a spear that had been jammed into some sort of cog system. "Dare I ask what this is?" he asked, touching the tip of his finger to the wickedly sharp point.

"Ah!" Lottie beamed. "I was trying to improve the way large clocks work by implementing a better spring system."

Thomas nodded, wishing he understood. "And the spear?"

"Oh," her smile dimmed a bit. "It worked so well that the clock started to run fast, so fast that the parts began to fly off. The spear was the only way I could stop the cogs." She shrugged and added in a whisper, "don't tell William, but I stole the spear from one of his ancestral suits of armor."

After Lottie showed him some of her other inventions, a maid came panting up the stairs to inform Lottie that it was time for her to get dressed. The guests would be arriving soon. Thomas bid her farewell and promised to bring the rest of the boxes and barrels up to her laboratory.

As she walked away, Thomas stared after her in wonder. Listening to her talk about her inventions was like watching a fairy weave magic and create a new world, one that Thomas desperately wanted to belong in. He realized with a sinking feeling that he could happily listen to her talk about her inventions for the rest of his days.

"Oh," Lottie paused at the door to look back at him with a devious grin. "Do be careful with those boxes and barrels. They're a bit... sensitive."

Thomas raised his brows, wondering if William's prediction about his life being in danger really wasn't a jest after all. "Dare I ask what's in them?"

"Firework and black powder," Lottie winked and dashed down the spiral staircase with a giggle.

Thomas gulped.

***Thomas stooped to lift the last of Lottie's parcels from the side of the stable entrance. He'd carried the rest up the long spiral stairs to avoid using Lottie's pully system, and the dizzying heights of the castle walls.

The sounds of hoofbeats made him pause and look up. A man led a dark bay horse to the stables, his hat pulled low over his eyes.

"Take care of this, stable boy," the man slapped the reins into Thomas's hand, making him fumble the box.

Thomas barely managed to catch the box in time and set it back down carefully. He bit his lip to keep from scolding Lord Greyville's guest and turned to go.

"I thought I recognized you last night," the man said, raising his head to reveal his face.

It took Thomas a moment to recognize the sunken eyes and cheeks. He tightened his grip on the reins and sorely wished he had some sort of weapon. "Mr. Farraday."

"A pleasure, Thomas Hawthorne. Or should I greet you as..." Mr. Farraday swept his hat off his head and bowed elegantly. "M'Lord?"

Crazy Fidelia

There were two men that Lottie had already placed on her list of the most disgusting people on the earth, and she believed she had just met the third.

Lottie and her dearest friend, Octavia Palmer, stared in horror at Sir Roland, who stood across from them in the sitting room of Lambert Castle. He was an older man, perhaps in his fifties, with reddish-blond hair, beady eyes, and his finger stuck up the nostril of his bulbous nose. He attempted to hide it behind a handkerchief, but Lottie and Octavia could clearly see it.

"Fascinating," Octavia whispered, her upper lip quirked in intrigued disgust. "Do you suppose he'll reach his brain at this rate?"

Lottie snorted and slapped a hand over her mouth to hide the sound. Lottie and the Countess had greeted the house party's guests in turn when they arrived in their carriages, and the large group now awaited the bell summoning them to supper in the dining room. Fidelia, the Countess's daughter-in-law, should have been there to greet the guests upon their arrival, but she'd claimed ill and begged off. Now, Lottie's redheaded sister stood beside William at the front of the room, her smile obviously strained as she listened Lady Hillington discuss her second son's recent return from the Navy.

Lottie elbowed Octavia in the side good-naturedly. "The Countess always says that every house party must have at least one insufferable guest. William said he hates to invite Sir Roland but he's a beloved fixture in the neighborhood. No one really understands why."

Octavia's lips twitched. "Careful, my dear Lottie, if the Countess hears you talking like that, she'll pair you up with him for supper. I'd wager you'd have a marriage proposal before the night is through."

Lottie gagged at the thought. "Don't remind me. The Countess has been throwing me at every eligible man with good standing in sight."

When the war had been declared between America and England in June of 1812, Lottie and Fidelia had been trapped in the ensuing riots that raged through Baltimore. A greasy Frenchman, Monsieur Le Coquin, had tried to kidnap Lottie during the commotion, but Lottie's brother Charles had sent William, to rescue the Atwell sisters. To escape Le Coquin, they had been forced to flee aboard a ship bound for England with William.

It had been Octavia Palmer and her father, a British merchant forced to flee back to England, who had first spotted William standing closely with Fidelia on deck. To preserve her honor, William had claimed that Fidelia was his wife. Although their marriage had started out like two dogs snarling and biting at each other's tails, love had soon blossomed between the two and they were now living as a nauseatingly affectionate couple. Meanwhile, Lottie had found a dear friend in Octavia, and they had been practically inseparable since then.

The door to the room opened and Lottie looked around, expecting to see one of the servants announcing supper, but she froze in shock.

"Mr. Farraday," she whispered, wrapping her hands around the folds of her skirts to hide their trembling. He had come after all.

"Forgive me for being late," Mr. Farraday announced to the room, and everyone turned in surprise. His gaze flitted around the room before finally resting on Lottie. She shivered as he pulled his lips up into a greasy, weasel-like smile.

William and Fidelia approached Mr. Farraday to exchange greetings and Lottie wondered with panic how they knew each other. How had he managed to secure himself an invitation?

After their pleasantries were over, Fidelia quickly pulled William away and Mr. Farraday moved on to stand next to Mrs. Ashdown and her niece, Miss Wilde. The two cowered as the newest guest leered down at them, taking Miss Wilde's hand and kissing it. Mrs. Ashdown was the recently widowed wife of a local gentleman and an even bigger gossip than Octavia. Lottie had had the unfortunate opportunity to interact with the woman on multiple occasions over tea and visits in the neighborhood, and each time the woman had criticized Lottie for every fault she could find.

Her niece, Miss Wilde, had recently returned from living in the Caribbean on her father's plantation, and Lottie had already been barraged with 'oh, doesn't she look lovely?' and 'exactly how a young lady should look. She'll certainly snag a handsome and rich husband' in the short amount of time that Mrs. Ashdown had been at Lambton Castle.

Keeping one eye on Mr. Farraday, Lottie circled the edge of the room to find William and Fidelia. She had to warn them about their new house guest. Fidelia was engaged in conversation so Lottie tugged on William's sleeve, pulling him aside.

"What's wrong?" he asked, blinking in surprise at her expression. "You look like you've seen death itself."

"I think I have," Lottie whispered, looking around to ensure that no one could hear them. "William, I have to tell you something. It's... well, maybe not urgent quite yet, but it might be—"

"Is it something that would worry Fidelia?" William asked, and Lottie noticed for the first time how anxious he seemed. Normally, William stood tall, even with his cane and mangled leg, and spoke with an air of confidence. Now, he kept fidgeting with his cane and glancing back every other second to his wife.

Lottie's heart tightened with fear. "Yes, but that's exactly why I should tell you—"

William raised his hand to cut her off. "Then please don't say anything here. Fidelia mustn't hear anything about this. She's... already been acting strange enough as it is."

They both turned to look at Fidelia, who, Lottie had to admit, looked awfully pale, even in the candlelight. "What's wrong? Is she ill?"

Her brother-in-law opened his mouth but paused, then he shrugged. "I... I think so. She hardly eats anymore, and when she does it's the strangest things like pickled eggs and even pieces of chalk. I frequently find her wandering the halls at night, muttering to herself. She's even started hiding food in weird places, like a squirrel."

Lottie's lips twitched even as she agreed that Fidelia's list of symptoms was alarming. "She's... hiding food?"

William nodded and threw one hand up in the air in exasperation. "Amongst other things. I found an entire loaf of molded bread wrapped up in my best pair of trousers this evening, and a block of cheese in the chest at the foot of our bed. She's also started stashing knives in the bed. Knives, I tell you."

Heart sinking, Lottie realized that she may have make Mr. Farraday leave on her own. Just then, a servant announced that supper was ready. Much to Lottie's dismay, the Countess led Sir Roland over and announced that they would be paired for supper, entering after Lord Campbell and his sister Miss Campbell.

Sir Roland extended his hand, the one that had only recently vacated his nostrils, and she cringed at the sight. Why the rules of society expected Lottie to take his arm after what she had witnessed was beyond her. Biting her tongue to keep from gagging, she allowed him to lead her into the large dining room. Lottie glanced back to see that Octavia followed not far behind on the arm of Captain Hillington, Lady Hillington's son who had recently returned from the Navy. Octavia blushed and seemed rather pleased at her dinner partner.

"I hear you enjoy pretending to invent," Sir Roland began, resting his elbows on the table as he ate.

Lottie choked on her spoonful of the first course. She could handle his table manners, but how could he open the conversation in such a crass way? "I don't pretend, Sir Roland, I am an inventor."

"Don't be silly, Miss Lottie. Young ladies are only suited for embroidery or perhaps a basic book. Invention and science are reserved for those of stronger constitutions and mental capacity," Sir Roland chortled and looked around the table for support.

Lottie stared at him, her spoon halfway to her mouth. "Are you implying men?"

Sir Roland nodded as if pleased that she had understood his 'complicated' and 'elegant' words. "Just so. The stronger sex has the brains and the brawn, you understand. The weaker sex is best suited for birthing children and preparing meals."

"I see," Lottie quipped, struggling to contain her anger. "You must be a very good cook then, Sir Roland, since you declare your place to be in the kitchen. I do hope you will bring me a meal while I'm working in my laboratory."

Miss Catriona, who sat on the other side of her older brother, giggled. Lottie peered around Lord Campbell to see the young lady was scribbling in a small notebook in her lap. How she had managed to sneak it out while sitting next to her brother, Lottie would never know, but she had to admire the girl's tenacity.

Sir Roland dropped his spoon and blustered, his face a ruddy purple, highlighting the veins in his bulbous nose.

Lord Campbell leaned forward to head him off. "Fret not, Sir Roland, Miss Lottie is only a woman, after all, she does not understand your sense of humor or your intelligence," he said, winking at Lottie as if he had just done her a huge favor.

Lottie strangled a squeal of frustration. Apparently, this handsome man thought she would appreciate his verbal backhanded slap. "Oh, don't worry, Lord Campbell, I understand Sir Roland perfectly. While the two of you struggle to comprehend the basic vocabulary of your primers, I shall dedicate my next invention to you. Perhaps, after years of study, you may one day be able to understand the difficult concepts of my science."

The table fell silent and the Countess gasped in horror.

Cheeks burning, Lottie looked around at the faces staring at her.

Well. This house party is going swimmingly, isn't it? Lottie thought ruefully. She looked toward Fidelia for help, hoping her sister would see her distress.

Instead, Fidelia's face was pale and sweaty. She stared back at Lottie with unseeing eyes, seemingly unaware of her surroundings.

"Fidelia?" Lottie asked, throat tightening. Was this part of the illness that William had spoken of? William followed her gaze to his wife, who sat by his side.

Just as William reached for her hand, Fidelia lurched to her feet and swayed. "Pardon—" she slapped a hand over her mouth and stumbled. She only made it two steps toward the door before her knees buckled.

A Witch's Prophecy

"Fidelia!" Lottie and William cried in unison. William was by his wife's side in an instant, catching her before she could hit the ground.

Lottie and the Countess rose, coming to Fidelia's aid as William carried Fidelia from the room, but once in the hallway, he waved them back. "Take care of things here," he ordered.

The Countess nodded, her lips pressed into a thin line. She took Lottie's hand and the young woman realized her adopted mother was trembling. They watched the couple vanish down the hall, and Lottie rose on her toes, trying to see if Fidelia had regained consciousness, but all she could see was Fidelia's limp hand hanging down over William's shoulder.

"What's wrong with my sister?" Lottie asked in a whisper. As she watched them, she realized that William had left behind his cane, and, strangely enough, his limp was barely noticeable as he carried his wife.

But the Countess seemed at a loss for words and only muttered a prayer before she guided Lottie back into the dining room.

The guests were whispering between themselves and pointing anxiously after their ill hostess. Everyone except for Mr. Farraday, that is. Lottie realized his eyes were fixed pointedly on her. Did he know something about Fidelia?

The Countess reassured the guests that everything was fine and urged them to continue with their meal. Fidelia was simply overly tired, she explained. But Mr. Farraday only smiled slowly at the statement, still watching Lottie.

Lottie was forced to listen to Sir Roland's self-righteous blustering for the rest of supper, interjected by Lord Campbell's frequent comments that were at first annoying, and then utterly ridiculous. Not only did he misquote a line of Shakespeare as being from the Bible, but he also insisted that the war with America was already over and that it had been hardly more than a few skirmishes.

Breathing a sigh of relief as the party finally rose to retire to one of the spacious sitting rooms for an evening of pianoforte, Lottie tried to extricate herself from between the two odious men. Honestly, the Countess must truly be desperate to marry Lottie off if she were paring the young woman with these two idiots.

Was Fidelia well? Had she woken up yet? Determined to sneak away, Lottie ducked behind Lord Campbell and made for the door.

Miss Catriona slung her arm through Lottie's and pulled her off to the side of the sitting room, shocking Lottie at the friendliness of the gesture. The younger woman looked to be barely sixteen, with doe-like brown eyes and thick black curls twisted into an elegant hairdo reminiscent of ancient Roman statues. It was the height of fashion, but Lottie's hair was too slippery to hold such a pile.

"Give me all of the juicy details, Miss Lottie," Miss Catriona whispered, pulling out her little notebook.

"I beg your pardon?" Lottie tilted her head as she looked around for Octavia to come to her aid. She needed to check on Fidelia, not exchange gossip! But Octavia was in deep conversation with Captain Hillington and looked completely smitten.

"Was Sir Roland as smelly as he looks? Did his breath reek of bad eggs?" Miss Catriona held up her pencil, her doe-eyes peering at Lottie over the top of her notebook. They glittered with mischief and Lottie tried to decide if it was endearing or frightening. "I was so hoping that I would be paired with him, but, alas—"

"I—You wanted to be near him? I— well, yes, his breath was quite wretched," Lottie said between giggles as she glanced furtively at the door. At least Miss Catriona was a delightful addition to the evening.

One of Miss Catriona's eyebrows quirked, and she grinned, scratching away with her pencil in her book. "Wonderful. That's just what I was looking for."

"Uh," Lottie began, concern for the young woman tickling her curiosity. "May I ask why you are so fascinated with that man? Surely... you're not hoping for a match with him... are you?"

Miss Catriona stared at Lottie for a moment before she laughed and rolled her eyes. "Oh, heavens no. Foul men like him make perfect fodder for my latest story. The best characters are based on real people, you know."

Lottie's jaw dropped in surprise. Surely Miss Catriona was jesting?

Miss Catriona continued with a wave of her hand. "Yes, dearest, I write novels. Witty, wicked little things that make you blush and are banned from good society. But don't tell my brother," she added with a wink.

Lottie's shock that the young lady would tell her something so scandalous warred with her disbelief. "Miss Catriona, when you make a first impression, you certainly don't hold back."

"I don't get out much, as I'm sure you've heard," Miss Catriona grumbled and eyed her brother sideways. Her face brightened when her gaze flicked to Sir Roland, who was currently looking around for a new conversation partner as Lady Hillington excused herself with a grimace. "Oh, pardon me, but I must dissect my latest victim."

Miss Catriona breezed away with a giggle that could only be described as wicked and Lottie stared after her. Octavia joined her side and Lottie clasped her hand tightly. "Octavia, I fear this house party is filled with lunatics."

Octavia sighed happily, her gaze fixed on the dashing figure of Captain Hillington. "Some are quite pleasant," she said dreamily.

Lottie elbowed her friend and they giggled together. Finally, Lottie said "Miss Catriona seemed to suggest there were rumors about her I ought to know already."

Returning to the ever-professional gossip, Octavia cleared her throat expertly. "Oh, it's a sad tale to be sure. If you thought your family was ripe with rumors, it's nothing compared to the Duke of Argyle's family. You've already met the eldest, Lord Campbell," Octavia nodded towards the man in question. "He's quite the rake, so I hear."

"That imbecile?" Lottie cringed. Why any woman would fall for his jumbled quotes and blatant disrespect for women, she would never know.

"You are a rarity, my dear Lottie," Octavia said seriously, "most women want a handsome face, not a brilliant brain. You are probably the only one who cares about a man's heart instead of his wealth."

"You do realize that you just lumped yourself in the list of shallow women who care more about wealth than love?" Lottie asked, only partially joking.

Octavia smirked and touched her cheek with a dainty hand. "My father has no sons. I'm most useful to him if I find myself a wealthy husband. Why else would I be blessed with such a pretty face?" She eyed Captain Hillington as if she had just found the perfect prey before she returned to the topic at hand. "As I was saying, Lord Campbell is well-known throughout the ton, but most people don't even know about his two half-siblings."

"Miss Catriona is his half-sister?" Lottie asked, looking between the two Campbells in question. Now that she thought about it, they didn't share many resemblances. "But who is the other sibling? How come they aren't here?"

Octavia leaned in closer, her glossy brown hair catching the candlelight in a way that would probably make Captain Hillington flustered. "Lord McCabe. He and Miss Catriona are the children of the Duke's second marriage. He went off to fight Napoleon on the continent and died there. Her mother died in childbirth, and the rumors say it was God's punishment because she was a witch. Once Lord McCabe left, Miss Catriona was basically abandoned to her own devices by her father and half-brother. That's why she is so... wild," Octavia said the word as if it were a gentler one than what she really wanted to use.

Feeling a twinge of guilt for having been quick to judge the young Miss Catriona, Lottie chewed her lip as she listened to Octavia. So, that was why Miss Catriona seemed to hold such a grudge against her half-brother.

The conversation brought a familiar ache to Lottie's heart as she wondered once again what had happened to her own brother. Where was Charles? Fidelia needed him here.

***As the night progressed, a strange energy seemed to twine around the house party, and all strings tied back to Mr. Farraday. Lottie watched as he made his rounds among the guests, first speaking to Lady Hillington, who grew pale and asked her son to escort her to her room as soon as Mr. Farraday left her side, then Miss Wilde, who was left shaking after their conversation, and then Sir Roland. Mr. Farraday somehow performed the miracle of stemming the tide of Sir Roland's crude, boastful remarks.

Lottie watched helplessly as Mr. Farraday harassed the guests one by one, too nervous to say anything. The Earl and Countess seemed too distracted with their worry for Fidelia to notice what was happening, and when a servant whispered to the Countess that a doctor had arrived, the Countess rushed from the room, her hands clasped tightly.

As the guests dwindled, Lottie's hackles rose when Mr. Farraday drew Octavia apart from the group and handed her a letter. Lottie finally gathered her courage to confront the man, but Lord Campbell beat her to it. He clapped a hand on Mr. Farraday's shoulder.

"Come now, old chap, let's have a chat," Lord Campbell said pleasantly, but his lips were tight, and his eyes narrowed slightly.

Lottie watched them leave through the door and looked back at her friend. "Octavia? What--?"

But Octavia's face glowed a sickly shade in the light of the fire and candles and she crumpled the letter in a tight fist. "That scoundrel. I'll make him pay," Octavia hissed.

Lottie's jaw dropped, but Octavia pushed past her as if she didn't see her friend, and suddenly Lottie was left alone with Miss Catriona. The dark-haired young woman sat on a chair by the fire, tapping her pencil against her chin. Lottie wondered for a moment if she gave off a similar, eerie aura when she wrote in her own notebook. Did she unnerve people as much as Miss Catriona unnerved her?

"Well," Miss Catriona said with a wicked grin. "What a fascinating evening. From the looks on their faces, I'd be willing to bet on something horrible happening during this party."

Goosebumps crawled up Lottie's arms and traced across her back. The young woman's words seemed like a prophecy, and her large black eyes seemed to glow as if she were in a trance.

"W-who's faces?" Lottie asked, looking towards the door that Mr. Farraday had gone through.

"Everyone. People's faces tell more than they think, you know," Miss Catriona's voice was oddly flat, and she stood, gliding across the floor until she stood nose to nose with Lottie. "Even yours, although you hide it better than most. You pretend to be one of them, but I think you, Mr. Farraday, and I, all know that you're nothing like the rest of them."

Lottie leaned away, finding Miss Catriona's piercing gaze and proximity unsettling. She forced a laugh. "What am I, then?"

"If my calculations are correct?" Miss Catriona paused, and then she giggled. "A killer."

The Blackmailer Demands

Lottie shuddered, but Miss Catriona blinked, and her eyes brightened as if she were suddenly coming out of her trance.

"I bid you goodnight, my dear Miss Lottie," she said, her voice light and childlike, nothing like the ominous tone it had held only a moment before. Miss Catriona skipped from the room, her skirts fluttering behind her.

The fire flicked, casting dark shadows around the now-empty room, and shivers raced down Lottie's spine. This truly was the strangest house party she had ever been part of, and she found herself sorely missing the simple, ordinary life she had led in Baltimore, cleaning tables at her family's eatery and daydreaming about science and inventions.

With her mind still churning, Lottie found herself climbing the spiral staircase to her laboratory. The door creaked on its hinges as she pushed it open, but then she froze,

"Mr. Farraday," Lottie stared at the man. He stood just inside the doorway, leering down at her. He'd been waiting for her as if he could predict her every move. "What are you doing in my laboratory? I demand that you leave this instant!" Lottie lifted her chin, praying that he couldn't see the way she trembled beneath his cold stare.

Mr. Farraday shook his head slowly, never taking his eyes off her. "Did you forget? We never finished our conversation last night. Don't worry, that stableboy won't be interrupting us this time."

"Leave," Lottie ordered again, pointing down the stairs, "or I'll scream."

He sighed. "You never learn, do you? If you scream, then I'll just reveal to everyone that I have evidence you killed Monsieur Le Coquin at Warren Mill eleven months ago." He held up a leather-bound notebook and waved it under her nose.

Lottie stiffened. "How...? How could you possibly know about that?"

"That is for me to know and for you to never find out. This notebook contains enough evidence of your crimes that you'd be hanged within a week and anyone who helped you could swing from the gallows as well. Your family will never be able to show their faces in England again for the shame of your disgrace," Mr. Farraday paused.

He turned and strolled around her laboratory, lazily eyeing her inventions. "The magistrate is quite a strict man, so I hear. He's got a nose like a bloodhound and once he gets on the trail, he never gives up until he catches his man. Or woman, as the case may be. Would you like to find out for yourself if the stories about this magistrate are true?" He picked up a spyglass that she had been reconstructing and turned it over in his hand slowly.

Struggling to breathe past the lump in her throat, Lottie followed him. There was no way he was bluffing, no one could simply have guessed the details of that cursed night when Le Coquin dragged Lottie into that mill. There were no witnesses, and no one in England would have known Le Coquin was there. Although he had infiltrated with a small band of

Frenchmen, they had been captured by William's men before the night was through.

"What do you want?" She asked quietly, clasping her hands in front of her to give the air of calmness.

Mr. Farraday finally turned, grinning at her. "That's more like it. You see, I've lost a great deal of money on an investment last year and I'm looking to recoup my losses. Your brother-in-law, Lord Greyville, has something that could serve quite nicely for my purposes."

Lottie swayed and she leaned against the table by her side. "No. Leave William and Fidelia out of this."

"Don't worry, they won't be hurt as long as you do as I say. If you try anything to escape me, however..." Mr. Farraday stepped closer until he loomed over her, his foul breath making her cringe. "Don't forget that they will suffer the most if your secrets are revealed. Lord Greyville will lose everything. To save his family honor and name, he could try to separate himself from you and Fidelia, but then that would be devastating to his wife, wouldn't it? And at such a delicate time, too..."

She dropped her gaze. He was right. Lottie had fought for so long to fit into her new world and family, but Fidelia had fought even harder. She had put her life on the line to stay by William's side... What would happen to them all if the world knew what Lottie had done?

Mr. Farraday sighed with long-suffering and held up the leatherbound notebook. "Silly girl. If you just do as I say, this little notebook, and all of the evidence against you, will be destroyed, and you will never hear from me again. Satisfied?

"What do you want me to do?" she asked, voice shaking.

"It's simple, really," Mr. Farraday said, caressing her jawline with fingers as long and spindly as a spider's legs. "Your adoptive mother is quite concerned that you have yet to receive a proposal, so I hear."

His touch filled her with revulsion, and she jerked her face away. "If you are proposing marriage, Mr. Farraday, I can assure you that I have far better prospects."

He laughed. It was a harsh sound like someone tapping on tin. "Oh, men with ample desires such as myself do not wish to be trapped by a marriage. No, I want something much easier for you to give. I wish to have the papers that Lord Greyville hides away in the secret compartment of his desk."

Lottie blinked, confused. "What does that have to do with a marriage proposal?"

Mr. Farraday pursed his lips in aggravation as if he spoke to a simple child. "After my first spy, a dimwitted little maid, failed to obtain the papers and was fired, Lord Greyville's valet will not allow anyone else into his rooms other than Lady Greyville, but he may make an exception for you. I will distract your brother-in-law with talk of marriage and you can sneak up to his rooms. Tell his valet that Lord Greyville sent you for the documents and it's simple as that."

Lottie clenched her fists. "Do you swear to destroy the evidence of my involvement with Le Coquin if I do what you want?"

Mr. Farraday's lip twitched but he nodded. "Upon my life."

Her guilt strangling her until she could only whisper the words, Lottie said "I'll do it."

***Her heart thumping so hard that she could feel the vein in her neck jumping, Lottie gripped her skirts to keep from tripping her as she jogged through the dark hallways of the castle. What if a servant saw her?

At William's door, she knocked, her hands shaking, and when the valet opened the door, Lottie quickly stated the lie that she had rehearsed on the way up. "Lord Greyville asked me to retrieve a letter addressed to Lady Greyville."

The valet's eyebrows rose but he nodded. He was a rather dull-looking man in his sixties whose pouchy cheeks spoke of far too many alcoholic drinks. Lottie brushed by him, forcing her shoulders back in a show of confidence. William's writing desk was suspiciously bare, and Lottie wiped her sweaty hands on her skirts. What would Mr. Farraday do if William had already destroyed the papers?

But perhaps William had only become suspicious after the previous attempt. Perhaps he had...

"Could you bring me a candle? I'm afraid it's too dark in here for me to read the handwriting," Lottie said to the valet, carefully keeping her back to him so that he wouldn't see the empty writing desk.

The valet grumbled but she heard him move away from the doorway. With nimble fingers, Lottie traced the surface and sides of the desk. Finally, in the top of one of the drawers, she felt a small lever. So, William had a secret compartment after all. Lottie almost wished that he had been smarter and just burned the papers instead.

The hidden compartment dropped down, spilling out a stack of letters and papers. Which ones did Mr. Farraday want? Lottie clutched them tightly and hesitated for only a moment before she folded the stack twice and stuffed them down her bodice. Fidelia may have won the battle against the Countess for pockets in her dresses, but Lottie had lost.

With a click, Lottie closed the secret compartment just as the valet returned with a candle. She faced him with a smile. "Thank you, but it seems the letter isn't here. Lord Greyville must have been mistaken."

The valet sighed, grumbling something about her distracting him from his nap, and escorted Lottie out of the room. The door closed behind her firmly, but she couldn't release her held breath. She felt as if she would suffocate, and not just because of her now extra-tight corset.

Once Lottie was a safe distance away from William's rooms, she paused near a window and pulled out the papers, searching through the contents in a shaft of moonlight.

Perhaps she could figure out what Mr. Farraday wanted and warn William after delivering the documents—

The air snagged in her lungs. The second letter that she had opened trembled in her hands until it finally slipped through her fingers and fluttered to the floor. No, Lottie repeated over in her mind. This... this can't be happening to us.

If Lottie handed even one of these papers to Mr. Farraday, he would know that William was a British spy in the service of the Prince Regent.

***Hey Guys!

Thank you so much for reading this chapter! If you enjoyed it, please be sure to vote and comment!

What do you think Lottie is going to do? What should she do? I'd love to hear your thoughts!

Fidelia's Secret

L ottie's eyes stung and she stumbled, tripping on her skirts as she neared the family's private sitting room. *Fidelia. I must tell Fidelia. She'll know what to do. She can fix this!*

The letters and papers were safely back in her bodice, but they felt like an anvil on her chest. What had she done? How could she have allowed Mr. Farraday to trap her like this?

Without knocking, Lottie blindly pushed the door to the sitting room. "Fidelia! Please, I need your—"

She broke off when she saw William's panic-stricken face. He stood across the room, speaking to an elderly gentleman who might have been the doctor that arrived after supper. The Earl and Countess sat on the chairs beside the fire, their hands gripped tightly with anxiety.

Fidelia lay propped up on the settee across from them, her face equally pale.

"What's... what's wrong?" Lottie's voice cracked and she pressed a hand to her bodice. Did they already know? Heavens, what must they think of her betrayal?

William ignored her, speaking instead to the unfamiliar man. "What do you mean my wife is ill?"

The man smiled, patting William on the shoulder roughly. "Fret not, M'Lord, Lady Greyville is indeed ill, but in the best way."

Fidelia interrupted them, finally looking away from the fire and to her husband. "I'm... pregnant."

Lottie slapped a hand over her mouth to hide the awful choking sound that escaped. Pregnant? Fidelia was pregnant?

William's face paled at first, and then he burst into laughter.

Fidelia reddened. "You're not allowed to laugh!" She crossed her arms and her lips turned down in a pretty pout. "That's not how this is supposed to go."

William wiped tears from the corner of his eyes and knelt beside his wife, taking her hands in his. "Fidelia, you awful, clever girl. I thought you were dying!"

Lottie watched as Fidelia first snarled in defiance, and then her scowl vanished, and the expectant mother burst into tears.

"How could you call me awful? I know my ankles are swelling, but still—" Fidelia blubbered.

Lottie stared. Her fiercely independent sister was blubbering. Like a fish. It was both beautiful and horrifying.

William laughed again, tears gleaming on his cheeks as he cut off Fidelia's cries and kissed her soundly. Then he pulled back and kissed her belly, touching it so lightly that Lottie wondered if he was afraid that he would accidentally hurt the tiny baby growing inside.

The Countess squirmed uncomfortably at the sight and looked at her own husband with a deep blush. Finally, she turned back to Fidelia with the biggest smile that Lottie had ever seen on her adopted mother. "I'm so happy for you, my darlings!"

The Early nodded, his chest puffed out in pride. "A grandson to carry on my line," he said with satisfaction.

Fidelia and Lottie opened their mouths to protest, but the Countess elbowed her husband in the side. "A granddaughter for me to spoil and dote upon."

Lottie sagged against the door, emotions warring inside of her as she watched the happy, peaceful sight before her. The Countess and Earl argued over the sex of the still unborn child while William traced shapes over Fidelia's stomach and talked animatedly as if the baby could already hear him.

Happy tears burned Lottie's eyes and she turned her gaze upon her older sister. Fidelia had fought so hard for so long, caring for Lottie and Charles after the death of their father, marrying a man she at first despised, and then Fidelia had fought off a French invasion and the betrayal of a beloved friend... and through it all, she had carved out a place to be happy.

Fidelia deserved this moment of pure bliss, love, and utterly disgusting dotting on the part of her husband.

But then the tears burned Lottie's cheeks as she remembered why she had come in the first place. How could she ruin this for her sister and brother-in-law? How could she let them feel even another moment of fear?

With a sinking feeling, Lottie quietly backed away until she was hidden in the shadow of the doorway.

Rage coursed through her veins until her hands shook. A feeling she hadn't felt since that night in the mill filled Lottie, white-hot and blinding until she thought she would burst.

Feral.

Savage.

Uncontrollable.

In that moment, she knew what she had to do. It was her turn to protect her family, no matter the cost. Lottie would stop Mr. Farraday that night or die trying.

*** Lottie found Mr. Farraday in her laboratory, waiting just as he said he would be. He stood by the fireplace, gazing into the yellow flames with a calculating expression.

"Why did you make me do this?" Lottie said, her voice flat and cold.

Mr. Farraday smirked and turned towards her, clasping his hands behind his back. "Ah, my lovely Miss Lottie. You've returned with my treasure, I see."

Lottie looked down at the folded letters and papers in her left hand. She laughed, a short, harsh sound that she had never heard from herself before. In Lottie's right hand, she gripped the handle of her brother's knife, keeping the blade tipped up behind her arm so that Mr. Farraday couldn't see it. "Yes. I've brought what's yours."

"Come now, let's have it," Mr. Farraday flicked his fingers expectantly.

Finally looking back up at him, Lottie drew a deep breath. She advanced slowly and he turned, following her progress until she stood between him and the fire. "Why me? Why didn't you go to William or Fidelia with your threat?"

Mr. Farraday clucked his tongue and shook his head. "I knew you were a silly little thing, but don't you think you're taking this too far? Just hand over the papers."

Lottie held the papers up to the side, just out of Mr. Farraday's reach. "Tell me," she snapped.

He rolled his eyes in exasperation. "Oh, alright. I'll humor you. Why didn't I try to blackmail Lord Greyville or his wife? Well, everyone in England knows of your sister's fierceness. She is a rare type of woman, the kind that would rather die than bend to someone else's will. I knew the moment I heard the stories that she would be more of a threat to me than a golden goose. I do admit that I contemplated taking the matter to Lord Greyville," he tipped his head side to side thoughtfully. "But once I met him, I knew that his amicable façade hid a fierce determination equal to that of his wife."

The papers began to tremble in Lottie's tight grasp. "You thought I was an easy target?"

"Yes," Mr. Farraday nodded in satisfaction. "You are just the weak little sister of a brave woman who has done everything for you. She had shielded you your entire life, even at the expense of her own happiness. You are nothing compared to your sister."

"You're wrong. I am the shield now." With that, Lottie tossed the papers and letters behind her and into the fire. She knew they caught fire when the laboratory brightened in a flash.

"No!" Mr. Farraday snarled, lunging forward.

Lottie flipped the knife's handle over in her hand and swung it forward, the blade passing through the air with a hiss.

Mr. Farraday halted with a gasp; the sharp tip pressed against the base of this throat. "What are you doing?" he growled as he raised his hands.

"What I have to," Lottie responded, pressing the tip harder against his skin. "Give me the notebook."

Slowly, Mr. Farraday began to chuckle. "Silly girl. Did you really think I would bring my evidence with me? I knew that you were just the idiotic, weak little sister always living in the shadow of her siblings, but I expected a little more from you than this."

"Give it to me!" Lottie shouted and her hand began to tremble.

Mr. Farraday glanced at her shaking hand and his smile grew. "Truly, I don't have it on me. See?" He turned out his pockets and opened his waistcoat.

Lottie swallowed hard and her heart sank. The crackling sounds of the papers burning in the fire behind her were beginning to die. At least she had bought enough time for any proof of William's secret identity to crumble to ashes. The father of Fidelia's child would be safe. For now.

Taking advantage of her momentary distraction, Mr. Farraday carefully pushed the blade away from his neck. "What a shame. Now I must truly ruin you. You see, the evidence is with my trusted associate, someone hidden here among your guests that you'd never dream of suspecting. Should anything happen to me, all of your secrets will be revealed anyway. Imagine your family's disappointment in you. Poor girl. You were nothing before, but are you prepared to know what's below that?"

Lottie's shoulders sank and she lowered the blade. Mr. Farraday shoved her towards the door and his touch brought back that white-hot fury. She glared up at him and Mr. Farraday's confidence seemed to falter under her ferocity.

"Monsieur Le Coquin caused his own death through a fatal miscalculation. I advise you not to make the same mistake," she said as she slowly backed away from him.

"And what could that possibly be?" Mr. Farraday snorted.

"Do not underestimate me." With that, she turned and ran from the room.

Lottie raced blindly through the dark hallways, out through the castle's side door, and down the slope, until she suddenly found herself standing outside of the stable. Breathing hard, she came to her senses. Somehow, her feet knew exactly where to carry her.

She shoved the door open and paused just inside, trembling. Thomas, who was leaving one of the stalls with a pitchfork slung over his shoulder, looked up in surprise.

"Wee Lassie! What's wrong?" he asked, lowering his pitchfork.

Lottie pulled herself up to her full height, small as it was, and held out her knife. "Teach me how to kill a man."

***

FIDELIA AND WILLIAM ARE HAVING A BABY!!! We were all hoping they would, but what are your thoughts about it? I'd love to hear from you! Many of you guessed it, but thank you for not spoiling it for everyone else!

Fun fact: Fidelia's symptoms-- squirreling away food, craving chalk, etc. are common for pregnant women. Some women go into 'survival mode,' especially if they've experienced trauma in the past, and hiding resources or weapons for self-defense can be ways of protecting themselves during a vulnerable time.

Anyway, if you liked this chapter, please be sure to vote and comment!

Lessons In Murder

Thomas gawked at Lottie. "Are ye drunk?"

Her fierce expression faltered, and she lowered the knife. "N-no, I am of a sound mind."

"Oh, I doubt that," Thomas rested his pitchfork on his shoulder and closed the stall door behind him. "Unless it's a common thing for respectable young ladies to come to a man alone at night and request lessons in murder. Who knows? I have not been in society before, perhaps it's a new trend?"

Lottie's eyes, bright with unshed tears, crinkled at the corners and she finally laughed. She sniffed and pressed the back of her hand, which still held the knife, to her nose to stop it from running. "You never cease to amaze me, Mr. Hawthorne. This is a very serious matter; I shouldn't be laughing!"

Thomas grinned and paused in front of her. He ducked his head to be on her level, soaking in the glowing light of her smile. It was such a comforting sight. "Come, wee lassie. Something must be very wrong for you to come to me like this."

Lottie nodded, her gaze dropping. "I can't tell you who he is or what happened. It will only put you in danger. Just teach me how to kill him."

Thomas straightened. That same fear he'd seen in her eyes the other night had returned, only this time, she looked wild. Dangerous. Thomas knew she meant every word.

Lottie pushed past a confused Thomas and began riffling through the tack closet. She reemerged lugging a saddle far too big for her.

"What are you doing?" Thomas watched, bemused.

Lottie paused and blew the feathery bangs out of her eyes. "Saddle a horse, will you?"

"It's nigh midnight, wee lassie," Thomas folded his hands and leaned on his pitchfork. "Where are you intending to go?"

"Not me. We." she grunted. "Oh, fine!" She dropped the saddle on the floor and stood, pressing her hands against her lower back with a wince. "You're coming with me."

Thomas's eyes widened. "Oh, that'll be grand for your reputation."

Lottie glared at him, her pretty mouth pursed with determination. She hauled the saddle up onto her shoulder and attempted to position it on the back of Esquire, the large black gelding in the stall behind Thomas.

With a roll of his eyes, Thomas took the saddle from her before she could hurt the horse, or herself, and finished the job properly while Lottie retrieved two long winter coats for them. He led Esquire from the stall and presented it to the determined young woman. "There. Happy?"

"Get on," she pushed against his back with her shoulder, trying to force him up on the horse's back.

Thomas squawked. "Watch those hands, lassie! At least make a proposal before you touch me down there."

Lottie gasped indignantly. "I assure you my intentions are—you're teasing me again, aren't you?"

Thomas just winked. Lottie squealed in annoyance and shoved him in the backside again, straining to make him mount the horse. With a laugh, Thomas finally gave in and pulled himself into the saddle.

"Now lift me up, too," Lottie said, reaching her hand up expectantly.

"I beg your pardon? You want to ride with me?" Thomas drew the horse back a step, feigning alarm. "You have already taken advantage of me enough for one night, thank you very much."

She planted her hands on her hips and cocked her head in exasperation. "I can't ride. I haven't been able to since... since the mill."

"Oh," Thomas dropped his teasing smile and looked down at his hands uncomfortably. Le Coquin had thrown Lottie over the back of his horse and carted her off to the mill like a sack of potatoes. The memories of the experience must still haunt her. Silently, Thomas clasped her little hand in his and pulled her up onto the saddle in front of him.

"May I put my arms around you? I shall have to hold you on the horse." Thomas held his breath, concerned that his touch would make her uncomfortable.

Lottie turned to look up at him, her lips parting in surprise. "You are the first man to ever ask what I would be comfortable with. The first man to take my feelings into account before touching me," she said.

The words stunned Thomas into silence, and he stared down at her. Finally, all he could manage was, "I'm sorry."

She cocked her head and one of her blond curls came loose, tumbling down her back. "For what? You've done nothing wrong."

"I'm sorry that you've had to live in a world of men who think they own you," Thomas said. Lottie squeezed his hand in response and quickly turned away.

Thomas wrapped his arms around her, trying to keep his pulse under control, and they rode out of the stable and out across the snowy field towards the beach. They'd be far from prying eyes there.

Freezing wind blew drops of water from the ocean like needles against their cheeks when they arrived, but Lottie didn't seem to mind, so Thomas pulled Esquire to a halt and dismounted. He helped Lottie down and they walked together in silence for a long time before Thomas finally spoke. "You mustn't kill him, Lottie. Tell me what happened, and I can help."

Lottie grabbed Thomas by the arm and turned him to face her. Her cheeks were wet with tears, but her eyes blazed with anger. "Why can't I? This man knows what I did to Le Coquin. Why should I let this man threaten everything and everyone I care about?" she said, and her voice cracked. "I've killed before. What's one more ghost?"

Thomas placed his hands on her shoulders and bent to look her in the eye, praying that she would listen. "What you did to Le Coquin was in self-defense. The law and God are on your side, but the moment you kill someone else for any other reason, you are no longer justified."

"Justice?" Lottie snorted, shaking her head. "The law allows a titled man to kill another in defense of his honor or pride. If a poor man kills someone to defend himself or a loved one, then he is hanged as a murderer—" she broke off, pressing the back of her hand to her nose again.

Shaking his head, Thomas tried to understand why that example should be so personal to her, why she felt so afraid. How could he help her if she didn't tell him what was really going on?

Finally, Lottie looked away towards the pounding, freezing surf, and lifted her chin. "If a man hurts a woman, she is to blame. The woman is ruined, and the man is just a 'rake.' But if the woman should try to defend herself, her honor and pride, then she is punished by the law. She is punished once for 'enticing' the man and again for stopping him. Where is the justice in that?"

Thomas's heart broke at the desperation on her face. Lottie's eyes kept darting around as if she felt hunted, tormented by the fear this stranger had brought into her life. But even more than that, his heart hurt because he knew she was right. This was a world determined by powerful men, and women were just pawns to them.

Finally, he took a deep breath and let his hands fall away from her. "You're right. There is no justice in that. But the law will never change if we stay silent and take justice into our own hands."

Lottie stared up at him for a long moment and Thomas's heart wavered. She was striking in the moonlight, and her fierce expression filled him with both admiration and fear for what she might do. She said, "I wish I could be that brave and ideological... But I don't have that luxury. There are people that I must protect. I can't let them die. If I will not be justified, then so be it. If I must go to purgatory, then I'll take that man to the gates myself."

Lottie turned away and gripped Esquire's saddle. Silently, Thomas wrapped his hands around her waist and lifted her up onto the horse's back. Taking the reins, he walked by Esquire's head and guided Lottie back to the castle, keeping his eyes on the snowy path ahead.

When they returned to the stable, Thomas helped Lottie down and took her hand when she turned to leave. She looked up at him with questioning eyes, but he turned her arm over and slid the knife back out of her sleeve.

"If you must kill a man," Thomas said, turning the blade over until the tip faced his chest. He unbuttoned his coat and lifted Lottie's other hand, pressing it to his left collar bone. "Aim for the heart," he said, touching her fingers to each of his ribs as he counted down to the fourth and fifth bones.

Thomas slipped the handle of the knife into her hand and guided it to the right spot between the ribs. "Try not to hit the bones, or the blade will get stuck."

Face pale and but set with determination, Lottie nodded, tightening her fingers around the knife. Thomas slowly released her hands and they stood together for a long moment, Lottie staring at his shirt over his ribs in horror, and Thomas searching her face, desperate for another solution.

Finally, Lottie left, the long coat swirling around her as she fled back into the castle. Thomas stared after her until she vanished inside, and then he looked up to her observatory.

He would do anything to keep Lottie from making such a horrible deci sion... and it wasn't hard to know who was giving her trouble. Perhaps it was time for Thomas to take things into his own hands.

***

Hey Guys! Oooohhh Thomas is going to do something drastic! Any guesses as to what?

A bit of a shorter chapter because of my university finals, but what did you think?

Thank you for reading this far, and if you liked this chapter, please be sure to vote and comment!

What Happened With Edmund

L ottie tossed in her sleep, the same nightmares that had haunted her for a year chasing her once again, holding her hostage.

Lottie stood by the window in her room at the Thorpe's manor, straining to catch a glimpse of the handsome, tall blonde man who had captured her heart. Why did he want to talk to Fidelia instead of her? What were they talking about?

"Lottie..." a man's warm voice behind her made her heart jump in her chest and she spun around.

"Edmund!" Lottie couldn't hide her smile. Her heart always fluttered when she saw those merry blue eyes, the kind grin...

But something felt off about those eyes this time. "What... What's wrong?"

Edmund advanced toward her slowly. His left cheek was red as if he had been struck. When had that happened? He'd been talking to Fidelia only a moment ago...

He took her hand in his and Lottie went a little weak in the knees, remembering the way he had emerged from the darkness on horseback in Baltimore, swooping her up into his arms and rescuing her from her kidnappers during the riot. Edmund was a good man. A man she could dedicate her whole life and heart to. In her mind, she already had.

"Run away with me," he whispered urgently. "Right now, before Fidelia or William try to stop us."

The dream began to turn dark, her memories distorting as she smiled up at him and nodded.

Foolish girl! She tried to scream at her younger self as she watched the naïve girl turn and lead the way out to the servant's exit. No one would see them leave... no one could save her now...

"No! Don't go!" Lottie screamed, sitting upright in bed, fighting against the covers that wrapped around her legs and arms, suffocating her.

"Miss?" Sally, her maid, rushed in from the side room and lit a candle. Sally screamed at the sight of her mistress, but Lottie was too caught up in the fragments of her nightmare to register what was happening.

Someone threw open the bedroom door, but they stopped just inside with a gasp. "Lottie! Stop!" they cried, lunging toward her.

Lottie brought her arm down instinctively in defense and her attacker cried out, but they caught her wrist.

"Lottie, let go."

Breathing hard, sweat dripping down her forehead and the back of her neck, Lottie blinked. "O-Octavia?" she whispered, shaking her head in confusion. Slowly, she looked down at her hand.

Her knife trembled in her grip.

Octavia held Lottie's wrist tightly in one hand, the other brought up to protect Sally, who stood frozen in place just an inch from the blade's tip. Lottie had been about to slash her own maid in the midst of her nightmare.

With a gasp, Lottie dropped the knife. Octavia caught it deftly by the blade and flipped it over to grip it by the polished cherry handle in a steady hand. Octavia let out a slow breath and smiled uneasily. "You gave us quite the fright, my dear Lottie. Are you alright? What happened?"

Lottie closed her eyes, shaking her head again. "I'm so sorry, Sally, I-I don't know—"

"T'is alright, miss," Sally said gently and she helped Lottie sit down on the bed. "I've nay seen your night terrors this bad, miss."

"Do you have night terrors often?" Octavia asked sharply.

Lottie finally opened her eyes and looked up at her friend. She had rushed to Lottie's room dressed in only her nightgown, her lovely dark curls coming loose from a side braid. Octavia's gaze pierced into Lottie and she looked as commanding as a sea captain. She must have learned that from her father, Lottie thought absently, still trying to gather her mind.

"Every night. Every night for a year, I dream the same dream," she whispered.

Octavia bit her lip and looked at Sally. "Fetch some cold water, please."

Sally nodded and rushed from the room, twisting her apron anxiously. Sally knew better than anyone else, other than William and Fidelia, what had happened that night. After all, she had been the one to discover Edmund's ransom note stuck into the wall with Charles' knife.

"Why didn't you tell me?" Octavia asked gently as she sat next to Lottie on the bed.

"No one can know," Lottie said, staring at the wall across from her. "No one else can know what happened that night."

"That night—Lottie, what are you talking about? Dearest, please tell me—" Octavia began, clutching Lottie's hand tightly.

Something trickled between their clasped fingers and Lottie lifted their hands. "Octavia, you're hurt!" A long gash ran across her palm, warm blood oozing out.

Octavia blinked in surprise, turning her hand over to examine it. "Indeed, I am," she chuckled. "Fret not, dearest, I have seen far worse aboard my father's ship."

Lottie pushed to her feet. "I did that, didn't I?" She backed away, holding her hands to her stomach. "I hurt you."

Octavia smiled and shook her head. "It was an accident. You weren't thinking—"

Lottie panted, gasping for air. She had hurt her closest friend because of that terrible nightmare. She couldn't breathe. She had to get out of there. Turning, she fled from the room. In the hallway, she passed a frantic Sally who carried a large bowl of water. "Call for the doctor to tend to Octavia," Lottie ordered, hiccupping as she struggled to draw air.

She didn't stop to see if Sally obeyed, but only ran on. On down the hallway, down the stairs to the servant's exit and the grey light of the early morning hours.

Once again, she found herself standing outside of the stable, her mind too muddled to think clearly. Somehow, her body had known that Thomas was the only one who could help her. Lottie pushed the door open.

"Thomas?" she shouted desperately. "Thomas, where are you?"

But the stable was quiet. Lottie walked the aisle, looking in all the stalls in search of her Scotsman. Esquire's stall was empty, and Thomas was nowhere to be found.

Her mind still muddled, Lottie slowly collected a warm cloak and left the stables, pointing her feet towards the beach, hoping to find the same clarity there even if Thomas wasn't beside her this time. As she walked, thick snow began to fall and gather on the ground around her.

By the time she reached the beach an hour later, her mind was finally clear again, and it was time to plan.

Lottie chewed on her thumbnail as she walked along the beach, her mind racing. The sun barely began to peek over the edge of the ocean, turning the small waves golden as their tips caught the morning rays.

Lottie recalled the altercation she had had with Mr. Farraday the night before and the way he had threatened her. How did he know? Did he actually have any evidence? What could possibly be in that little notebook of his?

"I protected myself. How could that be so wrong? Why must I pay for the selfishness of a man who caused his own doom?" Lottie muttered. In her other hand, she clutched her little notebook of inventions so hard that the leather binding creaked. The leather cover was now stained with Octavia's blood which had coated Lottie's hand. Only the night before, she had held a knife in that shaky hand, pointing it at Mr. Farraday. "There has to be a way to stop him—"

Her toe collided with something firm, and she tripped forward onto the wet sand. Her notebook flew from her hands as she tried—and failed—to catch herself.

"Blast these skirts!" she spat out a mouthful of gritty sand and laughed ruefully at herself. Her adopted mother would likely faint at her foul language.

Lottie rolled over and sat up to brush off the fine blue linen of her skirts. They were already muddy and wet from the hour's walk from Lampton Castle, traipsing through the freshly fallen snow.

Then she spotted what had tripped her. Or rather, who had tripped her.

"M-mr. Farraday?" Lottie asked, touching his shoulder. "Are you alright.. .?" He was awfully pale, and his clothes were soaked, the rising tide lapping at the shredded remains of his grey coat fanned out around him on the sand. A dark red splotch stained his chest around a long, narrow cut.

Dread pooled in her gut and she scrambled backward with a scream. "Help! Somebody, help!"

But she was alone on the beach, and as her shock at the sight of a dead body drained away, a new thought made her stop shouting for help.

Someone had killed Mr. Farraday before she could.

But did that mean her secret had gone with him to the grave?

***

Lottie ran the whole way back to the castle through the snow, her heart lighter than it had been in weeks. Mr. Farraday was dead. Dead! Lottie was free! She had to tell Thomas. She could tell him everything now that the danger was passed and his life was safe.

Cheeks numb with the cold and her lungs tight and aching from running, Lottie sagged against the stable door. "Thomas!" she cried happily, pushing the door open.

The stable was so warm her fingers and toes stung as they warmed, and the comforting scent of hay and straw made her smile grow even larger. Everything was okay now. Everyone was safe, and the world seemed a brighter, warmer place.

Lottie reached Esquire's stall in a moment and looked over the door. "He's dead, Thomas. Dead! And I didn't even have to—"

Lottie broke off as she spotted Thomas. He was kneeling beside Esquire's left foreleg, examining the horse. He froze when he heard her voice and his broad shoulders tensed. Slowly, he stood and faced her.

Lottie gasped, covering her mouth at the sight of him.

Thomas was covered in blood.

***

Ooooh Things are not looking good for Thomas! Any thoughts on what he did?

What do you guys think of seeing what happened when Edmund kidnapped Lottie during the last book from Lottie's perspective? I'd love to hear your thoughts!

If you enjoyed this chapter, please be sure to vote and comment! You rock!

A Compromising Situation

Thomas's heart pounded at the sound of Lottie's voice behind him. What was she doing there at this hour of the morning? Could she possibly have found out-

He stood and turned slowly, shoulders tense. Lottie's bright eyes widened in horror when she saw him, and she covered her mouth.

At the same time, Thomas looked down at her hands. They were also covered in dried blood, and her skirt was stained with it, too, as if she had balled her hands in the fabric.

Losing all sense of propriety, Thomas grabbed her hands. "What's wrong? What's happened?" He turned her hands over, frantically examining them for injury. Had she truly confronted Mr. Farraday the night before? Was that why--?

"It's not my blood," Lottie reassured him, but then she shook her head. "Never mind that; what happened to you?" she gestured to his own blood-stained clothes.

Thomas sighed in relief. She was fine. But then his throat tightened. If it wasn't her blood on her own hands... whose was it?

"This?" Thomas looked down at his shirt, struggling to focus. "Oh. It's not mine, either."

They both laughed awkwardly, but then asked at the same time "Whose blood is it?"

They laughed again and Thomas gestured to Esquire behind him. "Some of the guests said they would go riding this morning and I took Esquire out to warm him up first. Unfortunately, he tripped in the snow and cut his knee quite badly. It's not dangerous, but leg wounds on horses tend to bleed like the dickens. I bound it with my shirt until we could get back to the stables." That was... partially true, Thomas grimaced.

Lottie's shoulders relaxed, but her brows still pinched together with concern. "What happened to your leg?"

Thomas followed her pointed finger to a large gash in his own leg, just below his knee. In his rushed state, he hadn't even noticed the torn plaid trousers, which were now missing a large chunk, and the bloody wound on his shin.

"Ah," he chuckled awkwardly. "I-I was thrown when Esquire tripped." That was true, but the gash had come later...

"Is Esquire alright now?" Lottie asked, peering around him nervously at the large black horse.

"Aye," Thomas returned to crouch by Esquire's leg and finished wrapping a dressing over the even stitches that Thomas had used to close the wound. "He'll be right as rain in a few weeks if we can keep the infection out."

"Good," Lottie said, taking Thomas by the hand and leading him into the back of the stables where his small room hid behind the tack room. She pushed him into a chair and filled his washbasin with fresh water.

The room was sparse, with only a bed, a chest for his clothes, and the washbasin and water pitcher. Even the ceiling of the room was unfinished, with the rafters leading up to the hayloft left exposed.

"Wee Lassie," Thomas protested gently, taking her blood-stained hand in his as she reached for a washcloth. "Ye ought not to be here. T'isn't proper."

Lottie lifted her chin, even as her cheeks tinged a delightful pink that made Thomas's heart constrict happily. "You belong to me, remember? How can you be a good guinea pig for my experiments if you get hurt or sick?"

Thomas grinned broadly and leaned back in his chair. Flitting his hand through the air, he said "Well, then, if it's for science..."

Lottie's lips twitched with a smile but then she pursed them with a professional air and rolled his trouser leg up to his knee. Cheeks still pink, she wrung the water out of the cloth before dabbing it gently against his wound. He hissed, finally feeling the pain that his adrenaline had kept at bay.

Wincing sympathetically, Lottie cleaned the wound with surprising deftness and wrapped a clean bandage-one of the many kept in the tack room for the horses-around his leg. She tore the end into two strips and twisted them over each other. Then she wrapped them around his leg again and tied them off.

"How do ye ken field dressing so well?" Thomas asked with a note of teasing in his voice. He quite enjoyed the way she fretted over him and carefully bandaged his wound.

"Fidelia is quite accident-prone, I'm afraid. I've cleaned many cuts and scrapes for her since our father passed away. He taught me how..." her voice trailed off for a moment and her eyes darkened. But then she shook her head and forced another smile.

Thomas's teasing mood faded at the sight of her pretending that nothing was the matter. It seemed as if she were always putting on another mask to appear the beautiful, dutiful debutant that everyone expected her to be.

He took her hands in his to stop her from fretting over the bandage. Taking a fresh washcloth from the pile she had collected, he slowly washed the blood from her hands. "What happened?" he asked again.

Lottie sighed and sat back on her heels. "I hurt Octavia on accident. I was having a nightmare, and I grabbed my knife... Octavia caught it, but I cut her hand."

Thomas nodded silently, continuing to clean her hands with long, smooth strokes of the washcloth. Crimson swirls darkened the water as he rinsed it again.

Lottie continued, her eyes staring into space above his shoulder. "It's been a year now. Why does it still haunt me? Edmund is dead and gone but I see him every night. He still comes for me. I still go with him. I can never change it."

Thomas nodded again. "Ghosts never seem to rest, do they?" he paused, trying to decide if he should let her continue. Would it help her heal if she could talk about it? Finally, he asked, "who was he?"

Lottie sighed. "The man who traded me to Le Coquin that night in Budle. He... kidnapped me from the Thorpe's manor while everyone was distracted caring for William's injury. I thought I loved him. He was my world, the first thought in my mind in the morning and my dreams at night... but I was just a means to an end for him. How could I have been so foolish?"

Thomas's hands slowed. "It's not your fault. His choices are not your fault."

Lottie looked up sharply, her blue eyes flashing with unshed tears. "If everyone knew what happened, they would say it was my fault."

"They don't matter," Thomas shook his head, holding her hands in his. "People will always tear down strong, beautiful things, and ye, wee lassie, are stronger than anything."

"But not beautiful?" Lottie sniffed with a teasing smile.

Flustered, Thomas brushed away the tears that finally tracked down her cheeks with the pad of his thumb. "Nay, lassie, not just beautiful. Glorious."

She giggled.

A knock sounded at the door and they both froze.

"Thomas? Are you in there?" a man's voice called through the door, knocking again.

"William!" Lottie gasped, and they both looked down at her clothes, suddenly realizing at the same time that she was only wearing a cloak over her nightdress.

Thomas reddened and slapped a hand over his eyes, sputtering with embarrassment.

"Hide me!" Lottie hissed, dragging him to his feet. He kicked the washbasin and dark red water sloshed over the rim, splattering the floor.

"Where?" Thomas whispered as William knocked on the door again.

Lottie looked around the barren room with frustration, planting her hands on her hips, and then her gaze flicked up to the rafters above. Her eyes brightened. "Quickly, lift me up!" and she wrapped her arms around his neck.

Thomas froze at the sudden embrace, but the moment was quickly ruined as Lottie attempted to climb up him as if he were a ladder. He grinned and shook his head. This woman would be the death of him, he was sure. He wrapped his arms around her legs and hoisted her into the air.

Lottie scrabbled for a hold but finally caught one of the beams and Thomas shifted his hands to her feet, pushing her the rest of the way up. His nose twitched with a threatened sneeze as the hem of her dress slapped him in the face.

"Sorry!" Lottie hissed, finally pulling herself up onto the beam.

Thomas pressed a finger to his lips, trying to hide a smile as Lottie laid down on the beam, tucking the edges of her dress under her legs.

Finally safe, Thomas tried to comb his mussed hair and opened the door, praying that William wouldn't look up and see his young sister-in-law hiding in his stable master's rafters. That would be the talk of the town. Right after Thomas's funeral.

William was just turning around to leave when the door swung open. He turned, rolling his eyes in annoyance. "At last! I was beginning to think you had gone mad. What was all that ruckus I heard?" he asked, peering into the room.

Thomas smiled awkwardly, trying to hide the washbasin of bloody water. "Just trying to clean up my wound. Esquire threw me this morning," he gestured down to his bandaged leg.

William arched one of his brows as if he still doubted Thomas's story, but finally, he shook his head and tapped his cane on the floor as if uncertain. "I've come for your help. Well, to give you a promotion, you could say."

Thomas cocked his head, trying to ignore the flash of white nightgown that slipped down a few inches into the room. "Aye? Is there a problem?" Did he know something about Mr. Farraday and Lottie?

William thought for a moment, tapping the side of his first finger against his lips. "Something strange is going on with Lottie. Last night my valet said she came into my room for a letter, supposedly at my request... but now all of my hidden papers are gone. I've had to fire the useless braggart for the compromise in my security, but now my biggest concern is Lottie."

Thomas froze. Lottie had stolen something from William's bedroom? His eyes flicked up towards Lottie in the rafters before he could stop himself. "Have ye asked her about it yet?" Thomas asked.

William bowed his head. "No. She has not been the same since the incidents in Budle last year. I want to protect her from this as much as I can, and I fear she would not tell me even if I asked. What Edmund did... his betrayal has made it hard for her to trust anyone," William turned slowly and looked Thomas, his striking blue eyes deadly serious beneath his heavy brow. "Except for you. For some reason, she seems to trust you a great deal."

"I'm not sure I understand," Thomas said, resisting the urge to look up at Lottie again.

"I have been watching my sister-in-law closely over the last year. Lottie hides it well, but she still lives in fear every day. At the balls, she looks physically ill whenever a man touches her. The only time I have seen her truly act like her old self was when you helped her take those boxes up to her laboratory." William shook his head, pacing the room in a small circle as he worked through his thoughts. "She touched you, willingly and without fear. She smiled so brightly that I could almost believe it was all behind us."

"Perhaps it is only because I saved her that night that she knows I mean her no harm," Thomas offered, forgetting for a moment that the woman in question was hiding above them in the rafters. In her nightgown. Covered in blood. William certainly would not trust him anymore if he saw that.

"Perhaps," William tilted his head to the side. "But I believe it could be more than that. Either way, something strange is happening in my castle and I need someone that I can rely on wholeheartedly. Someone that Lottie will trust enough to tell why she stole my documents. I am asking you to come work as my valet."

Thomas froze. Work in the castle? So close to Catriona and Lord Campbell? He would be discovered for sure.

As if seeing Thomas's hesitancy, William placed a hand on his shoulder. "Please, Thomas. I am asking you as a friend, for Lottie's sake. Fidelia's health is very precarious now and it is my duty to care for her, first above all else. I need you to protect Lottie."

Slowly, Thomas nodded. "Aye, William. I will protect her with my life."

***

Hi guys! Sorry for the late update, my health has not been great the last week, but I hope you enjoyed this chapter! If you did, please vote and comment!

Edmund Returns

Lottie's heart ached oddly at Thomas's promise. She didn't realize that William had seen through her carefully crafted façade the past year and hearing someone else say the truth about her fears somehow felt comforting. Even now, Thomas knew what happened with Edmund, but he hadn't look at her any differently.

Below the beam that Lottie lay on, William smiled with relief and patted Thomas's shoulder again.

"Thank you, old friend," William said. "I can only pray that Lottie will listen to you. Now, if you'll excuse me, I must get back to Fidelia. She's been quite ill this morning."

Thomas nodded and bowed slightly, keeping his head down until William left, limping heavily but his shoulders straighter as if a weight had been lifted.

Lottie sighed as soon as she thought William was out of the stable, finally relaxing her death-grip on the beam. With a squeal, she lost her balance and rolled off the side of the rough wood.

Warm arms caught her, saving her from what would have been a painful landing on the floorboards below. Her mussed blond hair tangled around her face as Thomas held her carefully and the air was temporarily stolen from her lungs at the surprise of falling. Surely, it had nothing to do with his tight embrace.

"Lottie!" Thomas gasped, "ye scared the life out of me, lass!"

Freeing one of her arms from the folds of her thick cloak, she pushed the hair out of her eyes and looked up to see Thomas peering down at her, his warm brown eyes wide with concern.

Her heart fluttered and her lips parted. Silently, they stared at each other for several long moments. How had William noticed before her that she felt no fear when Thomas touched her? Was it possible that her broken trust was beginning to heal?

Finally, Thomas's gaze flicked down to her lips and he reddened right up to the tips of his ears. Lottie had to bite back a smile as he set her down gently and took her cheeks in his coarse hands, turning her face side to side as he brushed loose strands of her blond hair back into place.

The moment was horribly intimate, but oddly enough, Lottie didn't mind.

"There," Thomas said with a satisfied smile as he stepped back to examine her. "Lovely as ever."

She patted her head, pleased with how well he had righted her messy hair. Thomas will make a doting husband to a lucky woman someday, Lottie thought before she could stop herself. It was like a slash to her heart, and she dropped her gaze.

Foolish girl, she chided herself, clasping her cloak closed around her shoulders. Who was she to be thinking about what Thomas would be like as a husband?

"What's the matter with Fidelia?" Thomas asked as if trying to break the awkward silence between them.

Lottie welcomed the distraction as she furiously commanded her blushing cheeks to return to normal. "Oh! It's the most joyful news. She's expecting a child! But she's been terribly ill because of it."

Thomas grinned, one side of his mouth pulling up more than the other in a way that made his face look boyish and cheery. "Aye, that's marvelous indeed. I recall my mother was also ill with my younger sister; I can see why William would nay want to trouble her."

Lottie's joy faded quickly as she was reminded of her original intention in coming to find Thomas. She touched his hand urgently. "Thomas, can you saddle a horse? I need to show you something at the beach."

***

Lottie rode behind Thomas on Caesar, one of the other geldings, her arms wrapped around his waist and her cheeks pressed against his back to hide from the frigid wind. Riding a horse was certainly easier in boy's trousers—she had borrowed a set of Thomas's clothes and cap after he pointed out that it would cause quite a stir if she was recognized riding off with him, especially in a bloody nightgown.

Thomas seemed a little on edge as he drew the horse to a halt at the top of the knoll overlooking the beach. "What is it ye wanted to show me?"

Lottie slid off the side of the horse and landed unevenly. "I think someone has killed Mr. Farraday," she explained, leading the way down the grassy hill. "I found him at sunrise right—"

She broke off and stopped. The body was gone! "I... I don't understand. He was right here," Lottie said, pointing to a bloody patch on the sand, the waves already starting to lap at the edges as the tide came in.

Thomas relaxed slightly. "Are ye certain, wee Lassie? It was dark, perhaps it was an animal—"

Lottie rounded on him and glared. "I'm certain. I fell right on him and saw the bloody gash on his chest. His coat was shredded like he had been attacked. Could the tide have carried him away?"

Thomas opened his mouth but hesitated. Finally, he tipped his head to the side, examining the sand. "Nay, the tide is only just coming in. But look here," he knelt and pointed to where the waves were creeping closer to the bloody patch. "There are two grooves here, leading towards the ocean... like someone dragged the body into the water."

"But why would they do that?" Lottie shook her head in confusion.

"To hide their tracks. It would be easy to follow if they dragged it across the beach. Either the body is still in the water, or they pulled it out somewhere else along the shore to hide it again." Thomas shrugged and stood, brushing the sand off his trousers.

Lottie thought for a moment, nibbling on her thumbnail. "Something is not right about this..."

"I should say so," Thomas said with a grim chuckle. "A man has been murdered and the body stolen. Ye have quite the knack for strange circumstances, wee Lassie."

Lottie reached for her notebook as her mind raced. She needed to write everything down before she forgot the details— but her notebook was not in her pocket. Perhaps she had left it with her nightgown back in Thomas's room. But she pushed that issue aside for a moment and focused on the sand again.

"We should leave, wee Lassie," Thomas said, touching her arm gently. "William is expecting me, and your family will worry if you are gone any longer."

Lottie nodded slowly. "I suppose it's no great loss if the body is not found," she said ruefully. "Mr. Farraday was a coward who prayed on other people's secrets to torture them. Now that he is gone, my loved ones are safe. Let him rot for all I care." She turned on her heel so quickly that the long cloak flared out around her. She was glad to be rid of that blood-sucking leech. It wasn't her business who killed him.

It wasn't her, after all.

*** After returning to the castle, Lottie and Thomas parted ways at the servant's entrance and he promised to look for her notebook and bring it to her later that evening.

The guests seemed oddly chipper when Lottie finally entered the breakfast room an hour later, Sally having cleaned away any evidence of her morning escapades.

"You seem very happy," Lottie whispered to Octavia as she sat. A servant served her plate and Lottie's stomach growled at the lovely scent of breakfast.

Octavia smiled coyly. "Captain Hillington has invited me to stroll along the gardens this afternoon," she said with a wink. "And, as if the heavens continue to send blessings for all of my good deeds, that odious Mr. Farraday has taken his leave!"

Lottie dropped her fork with a clatter, chipping the fine china plate. "Mr. Farraday... left?"

"Yes," Lord Campbell said, leaning across the table to join in on the conversation. "Mr. Farraday delivered a note to the Earl half an hour ago by courier which read that, regrettably, he had to attend to some family business and would not return for the rest of the party." He said the word 'regrettably' as if Mr. Farraday's company was no great loss to anyone.

Lottie swallowed the lump in her throat and her stomach twisted with unease. Mr. Farraday couldn't have delivered that note... he was already dead.

The door opened and William entered, pushing a wheeled chair in which sat a very angry-looking Fidelia. Her face was so red it nearly matcher her hair, and even her neck was splotchy. Thomas followed not far behind, dressed in a footman's lavish livery. Lottie caught her breath and had to admit that, from a purely scientific perspective... Thomas looked rather dashing in his black coat with gold trimmings, knee-length trousers, and complementary stockings.

Catriona, who sat on Lottie's other side, started in surprise, staring at Thomas. Perhaps she was also admiring how handsome he looked, Lottie thought, and it made her chest tighten with a sudden surge of protectiveness towards her Scotsman.

After the guests greeted William and Fidelia, Lottie rose and clasped her sister's hand, doing her best not to stare at Thomas, who stood back a few steps, doing his best to blend in with the other footmen. He failed miserably, however. Those broad shoulders were hard to hide.

"You look... lovely?" Lottie whispered playfully to Fidelia.

Fidelia's shoulders slumped, and she squirmed in the large, wheeled chair. "I look utterly ridiculous. I told William I was fine, but he insisted—"

"The doctor ordered you to rest as much as possible," William interrupted, kneeling beside Fidelia to adjust a thick blanket on her lap. "And I will not be moved on this matter."

Lottie giggled.

"Save me, Lottie," Fidelia whispered, looking up at Lottie with begging eyes. "I'm about to suffocate!"

"From the mound of blankets your husband is piling onto you? Or from his doting?" Lottie responded with a grin. "I've never seen a grown man fret so much."

"Both!" Fidelia grumbled, but Lottie spied the small smile that played on her lips as William again checked to see if she was comfortable.

Lottie left them to their adorable, and slightly sickening, affection for each other and stood discreetly near Thomas. "I thought you were supposed to be William's valet, not a footman," she whispered out of the corner of her mouth.

Thomas shifted uncomfortably, his powdered wig sliding sideways slightly. "The housekeeper and butler said it was improper for a valet to accompany Lord and Lady Greyville... and, apparently, the housekeeper desperately wanted me to wear the livery to 'blend in better.'"

"Ah," Lottie said with a knowing grin. "She must have liked your calves. It's a defining trait of a footman, so I hear."

Thomas coughed and his cheeks reddened. "I believe the word she used to describe mine was... delicious."

The footmen on either side of him twitched with repressed laughter.

*** The rest of the day passed pleasantly now that Mr. Farraday's fowl fog had lifted from the company, but Lottie couldn't shake the feeling that something was wrong about the situation. Mr. Farraday was dead. She had seen it with her own eyes. Someone had moved the body and delivered a note to the Earl to excuse Mr. Farraday's absence...

Lottie sat in the family's private sitting room late that evening after everyone had gone to bed, staring into the fire. She would have felt better if she could write everything down, but Thomas had said her notebook wasn't left with her nightgown, and she couldn't find it anywhere in her rooms.

"Miss Lottie?" Sally knocked on the door and stepping inside, wringing her apron as she often did when something was amiss.

"Hmm?" Lottie looked up, blinking away her confused thoughts. "Is something the matter?"

"It's Fidelia," Sally said awkwardly. "She's... walking the halls alone. She doesn't seem herself, miss."

Lottie stood quickly and followed Sally down the twisting corridors, her heart in her throat. Fidelia needed absolute rest, what was she doing walking alone at night? What if she got hurt? What if something happened to the baby?

Sally led Lottie into the main foyer of the castle and pointed towards the door, her hand shaking.

Fidelia wandered aimlessly along the red rug towards the door, the wind howling against the wood as a blizzard raged outside. She looked like a painting Lottie had seen once of a Banshee, her white nightgown glowing eerily against the blood-red curls that cascaded freely down her back. She seemed to float across the floor, her chin tipped up and her eyes unfocused.

"Fid--!" Lottie began to shout, but an arm wrapped around her shoulders gently. She jerked in surprise.

Thomas held a finger to his lips and then slowly pointed back to Fidelia. William appeared from the shadows and paused at the sight of his wife. He took a deep breath and strode towards her, his limp less pronounced than it had been the past few days. William's hair, loose from its usual tie at the nape of his neck, swung forward as he dipped his head to look in his wife's eyes.

He spoke to her softly, taking her hand carefully in his. From her vantage point, Lottie could see as Fidelia started in surprise and blinked rapidly as if waking from a dream.

"William?" she whispered, looking around in alarm. "Where am I? Where's Lottie?"

"You're with me, my clever girl," William responded, tucking a curl behind her ear. "At the castle. Lottie's fine. She's safe now."

Fidelia shook her head and tried to pull away. "I have to go. He's got her. I have to get to Budle and stop him—"

William pulled her into his arms and held her to his chest. "Shh, my darling," he whispered against her hair. "It was just a dream. Edmund is gone. I'm here now."

Fidelia struggled for a moment, but then she melted against him, grabbing his shirtfront with both hands as she leaned her forehead against his chest. "I did it again, didn't I?"

Lottie blinked and turned her face into Thomas's shoulder, anger heating her cheeks as she realized that Fidelia seemed just as haunted as Lottie was. This was all Edmund's fault. How could he continue to torture them like this?

Thomas tightened his arm around her shoulders and cupped his hand against the back of her head. How could such a simple touch be so comforting, Lottie wondered as she burrowed closer to him.

A thunderous knock pounded against the door.

Lottie jumped, grasping Thomas's coat. He pulled her closer and slightly to the side so he was between her and the door.

The knock pounded again, and William looked around for the butler, who had already turned in for the night. It was well after midnight, who would be calling at this hour?

The door swung open, pushed from the outside by their mysterious guest.

Snow swirled into the foyer, gathering on the stone floors as the wind moaned ominously. A cloaked figure stood in the doorway; a hat pulled low over his eyes to hide his face.

Lottie watched, stunned. William tensed and pulled his wife backward several steps as the intruder advanced several steps.

"Who are you?" William asked, his voice rough with anger. "How dare you—"

"Good to see you, too," the man said, sweeping his hat from his head. "Lord Greyville."

Fidelia screamed. She clutched at her stomach and collapsed.

"Fidelia!" William shouted, catching her, but his leg gave out as if their visitor also shocked him, and he sank to the floor with Fidelia, cushioning her fall.

Lottie stared and the ground dropped out from under her. She swayed.

"Edmund de Lacy."

***Hey guys!

I'm so sorry for the late update! I've been having a lot of problems with my heart so I spend most of my free time sleeping instead of writing, but I'm getting back into the swing of things! I promise to give you regular chapter updates from here on out.

Also.... EDMUND!!!! What do you think is going on? Is he really back?? What is he here to do?

I'd love to hear your thoughts!

Also, here is a picture of what Edmund looks like, in case you've forgotten or want to know.

Accused of Murder

Lottie shrieked with rage and launched at the intruder, clawing at his face and hands.

Edmund barked in surprise and raised his arm to block her attack.

"You!" Lottie screamed and threw his arm aside so she could slash at his face again. "I'll kill you myself, you coward!"

Edmund pushed her back and Lottie stumbled, tripping on her dress. The stone floor dug into her hip, but she didn't feel it. Red clouded her vision and she reached into her pocket, drawing Charles's small knife from its sheath.

"Lottie, wait!" Thomas shouted, but Lottie ignored him. She lurched to her feet, swinging the blade wildly at Edmund's chest.

He dodged her easily, an amused smile on his lips. His blue eyes, those eyes that had haunted her dreams for a year, glowered down at her. He snatched her wrist, twisting it slightly.

Lottie hissed in pain, dropping the knife and catching it with her other hand. She slashed at him again, the blade slicing through the edge of his cloak as he threw himself back.

Thomas grabbed her around the waist, lifting her into the air. "Stop!" he ordered, catching her arm when she swung blindly again. "Lottie, stop it! It's not Edmund!"

"Let go! I won't let him hurt us again!" Lottie writhed and tried the wrench her wrist free of his strong grip.

"Edmund?" the intruder asked, pushing away from the wall that Lottie had backed him into. He straightened his coat and smoothed his blond hair slowly. "Interesting..."

Lottie's struggles died and she sagged against Thomas, panting with spent rage. "You should have stayed dead," she seethed, glaring at the man.

The intruder smirked and stalked closer until he glowered over her. "My brother is dead, Miss Lottie. I have Lord and Lady Greyville to thank for that."

Lottie froze. "Your... brother." Slowly, the ringing in her ears faded and she realized that William was calling frantically for the footmen and the physician. "Fidelia," she breathed, pushing away from Thomas. Her knife clattered to the floor.

Fidelia lay on her side on the red rug, curled into a ball against a pain in her stomach. William smoothed her hair with shaking hands. "Fidelia? Oh, my darling," he whispered, moisture flashing in his eyes.

"What's wrong with her?" Lottie asked.

William shook his head, his eyes wide. The footman ran into the room carrying candles to light the way for the physician, who William had asked to stay for the next several days.

The physician knelt beside Fidelia and checked her pulse. He frowned. "Carry her to the family's sitting room," he ordered the footmen. "Quickly."

Fidelia's hand slipped from William's as the footmen lifted her and carried her away. He sat for a moment, staring after them in stunned silence. Then his face darkened.

Lottie sat back, her heart pounding. She had never seen him look so ferocious.

He launched to his feet and grabbed Edmund's brother by the lapels, pulling him off balance. "If anything happens to my wife or child," William hissed, pushing the man up against the wall, "I will tear you limb from limb, no matter whose brother you are."

Mr. de Lacy chuckled, his face entirely calm and so smug Lottie wanted to slap it. "That's no way to speak to the magistrate, now is it, M'lord?"

William snarled, but he seemed to recall who he was, and his position, and he slowly unfurled his fists. "I'm not finished with you," he said quietly. He turned and gestured to Thomas. "Mr. Hawthorne, please take our... guest to the library. I will see him when I ensure Fidelia is alright."

"Aye, M'lord," Thomas dipped his head. William nodded and limped after his wife.

Thomas straightened and stared hard at the magistrate. "Your Honor, if ye would follow me."

The magistrate narrowed his eyes. "Mr. Hawthorne, eh?" he rubbed his cleanly shaven chin thoughtfully. He nodded and gestured for Thomas to lead on.

"I'm coming too," Lottie said firmly, snatching her knife from the floor where she had dropped it. As she turned, she spied a flash of white, like the edge of a skirt, disappearing around one of the corners. Had someone else witnessed the altercation?

"Please do," the magistrate said with an air of pleasantry. "My visit centers around you, after all."

Lottie paused, rubbing her thumb over the handle of the knife. What could he mean by that?

***

Once settled in the library, Lottie stood beside Thomas, staring at Edmund's brother, who sat in a chair beside the fire, calmly sipping a cup of tea brought by a sleepy maid. The resemblance was unnerving, Lottie thought with a shudder. But the more she examined him, the more she could see the differences. He was older, to be sure, perhaps in his early thirties, and his eyes had a harder edge to them. His hair was darker than Edmund's platinum blonde, and his shoulders broader.

Lottie opened her mouth to interrogate him, but Thomas nudged her and shook his head.

An hour of awkward silence later, William opened the door. He looked ragged, his hair unkempt and his clothes rumpled, but he straightened his shoulders when he spotted Edmund's brother.

"Arthur de Lacy," William said, reaching out his hand to properly greet his guest.

Mr. de Lacy stared at the hand for a long moment, then his gaze flicked up to William's face. "M'lord," he dipped his head but ignored the out-stretched hand.

William let out his breath slowly, and Lottie could tell he was struggling to maintain his composure. "To what do we owe the great honor of your company?"

"I have always questioned your explanation for my brother's death," Mr. de Lacy said, rising to stand by the fire. "'Killed in the service of His Majesty. An honorable death defending the lives of Lord and Lady Greyville against an assassination attempt at the hands of the French.' That was the explanation you gave my family, don't you recall?" He turned back to William and his lips twitched, but Lottie thought it looked more like a scowl.

William stiffened. "Edmund... was a dear friend. We continue to mourn his loss."

"The reaction I saw today was not that of friends mourning the death of the man who saved their lives. Miss Lottie has even sworn to kill me," Mr. de Lacy turned his glare onto Lottie, who shrank closer to Thomas. "Would you care to explain, Lord Greyville?"

Lottie had never asked William what he had told everyone about Edmund's death. She had never wanted to know.

"My wife and sister-in-law suffered greatly last year during the assassination attempt. They are traumatized and not thinking clearly; I fear your resemblance to your brother has brought back memories of their ordeal and fogged their minds. Please forgive them," William said, his voice smooth and pleasant, but his eyes flashed.

Mr. de Lacy's jaw worked, and he drew a deep breath. "Sadly, that is not the reason for my visit. I received a most peculiar letter this morning from a young lad in the nearby village. When I questioned him about it, he said that he was paid a shilling a day to hold onto the letter, with the instructions that, should the money stop coming, he was to deliver the letter to me that same day."

Lottie clasped her hands together, the hairs on the back of her neck prickling.

"And what were the contents of this mysterious letter?" William asked.

Mr. de Lacy smiled, but it didn't reach his eyes. He withdrew the letter from his waistcoat and shook it open. "'Your honor, if you are reading this letter, then I have been murdered. As the Justice of the Peace for the town of Sunderland within Durham County, I trust that you will arrest my murderer and secure justice for me. Fret not, it shall not be difficult. Miss Lottie Atwell, the young charge of Lord Greyville, has killed me the day before you receive this letter. Sincerely, Mr. Jonathan Farraday.'"

Lottie's stomach dropped and she swayed again.

"This is absurd," Thomas put his arm in front of Lottie protectively.

Although Lottie appreciated the gesture, she pushed his arm away and lifted her chin. "I have done nothing to Mr. Farraday," she stated calmly even as panic rose in her throat.

"Then where is the man in question?" Mr. de Lacy challenged, holding up the letter.

William reached for it, but Mr. de Lacy held it back with a condescending 'tut-tut.'

"Mr. Farraday sent a letter to the Earl this morning stating that he had urgent family matters to attend to and had to leave," Lottie's voice wavered as she remembered the sickening feeling of tripping over a dead body. He had never left.

Mr. de Lacy's eyes narrowed. "You're lying. Where is he?"

"Mr. de Lacy!" William snapped. "I have excused your behavior thus far, but—"

Lottie's breath quickened. "I... I do not know. Truly." That was correct, at least. She didn't know where his body had been moved to.

Mr. de Lacy's jaw worked again. "Hmm. I have checked with every watchman stationed at the roads leading out of Sunderland, but none have seen Mr. Farraday, therefore he is still here. In the absence of a body, I cannot arrest you... yet."

"You shall not touch her," Thomas growled, "now or ever."

Mr. de Lacy's gaze darted to Thomas and his eyes flickered, but his face remained unreadable. "Oh? And what does a lowly footman have to say about it?"

Thomas's face darkened as he remembered his place, but he didn't lower his gaze.

"It was not me," Lottie said, touching Thomas's arm to make him stand down. "I swear. If... If something happened to Mr. Farraday, there were plenty of people here who had reason to harm him."

"Oh?" Mr. de Lacy's head cocked, amused. "And what would those reasons be?"

Lottie faltered and reached instinctively for her notebook, remembering too late that she still hadn't found it. "I... I do not know, but the guests were all terrified of him. When we learned that he had left this morning, everyone was relieved."

Mr. de Lacy stared at her thoughtfully. "Then I shall have to stay and investigate more, won't I?"

William stepped between them, his voice low. "I must protest your accusations, Mr. de Lacy. First, you accuse my young sister-in-law of murdering a grown man, and now you are accusing my guests? As you said, there is no body. The only evidence you claim is a letter that could have come from anyone."

"Are you trying to hide something from me, Lord Greyville?" Mr. de Lacy challenged, leaning closer to glare at him. "Something about my brother's death, perhaps?"

William's shoulders tensed. "What I told your family was the truth, Mr. de Lacy. There is not a day that goes by that I do not recall what Edmund did for my family," his hand tightened on his cane and Lottie winced.

What did Edmund do for them? He shot William in the leg and crippled him, perhaps for life!

"Then you won't protest in me staying to investigate for a few days?" Mr. de Lacy asked, and Lottie realized with a sinking feeling that he had trapped them.

William was silent for a moment, but then he nodded slowly. "Please do. I assure you that we have nothing to hide. But I urge you not to alert the guests that you suspect Mr. Farraday has been murdered. If one of them knows something, they will find a way to hide the evidence or cause the guests to all leave before you have the chance to stop them, and then you will have o way to learn the truth."

"Very well," Mr. de Lacy nodded, turning to stare at Lottie. "But rest assured, Lord Greyville, I shall leave no stone unturned. And when I have enough evidence to make an arrest, I shall, no matter their station or connections."

*** William ordered Thomas to escort Lottie back to her room while he saw to their new guest's accommodations, and Thomas struggled to maintain his composure as he walked beside Lottie.

How could the magistrate know so soon that Mr. Farraday had been murdered? Did Mr. Farraday really plan that far ahead, suspecting he would be killed?

But there was a bigger problem. All suspicion was now cast on Lottie. The thought made Thomas's blood roar in his ears. Did someone know what Thomas had done for her? Did they alert the magistrate to force Thomas's hand? He had done what he did to protect Lottie, not draw more attention to her.

Lottie stopped short just before her door.

"Wee Lassie?" Thomas asked, realizing she had grown even paler.

She snatched a folded letter from the ground, opening it with shaking hands. She gasped and the note fluttered from her fingers, drifting to the floor below.

"What's wrong?" Thomas picked up the dropped letter, forgetting all about Mr. de Lacy's accusations for a moment.

I still want what I came for, Miss Lottie. Do not try to escape me again.

--F

Thomas shook his head, reading the note again. "How is this possible? Mr. Farraday is dead. I—You saw his body!"

"It's not from him," Lottie said quietly, her voice firm with conviction.

"Then who could have written it?"

Lottie drew a deep breath and squared her shoulders. "Mr. Farraday's partner, the real blackmailer... the real killer."

Gossip and Black Powder

T homas took her shoulders, turning her to look at him. "Lottie, we should leave."

She blinked in surprise, the troubled look in her eyes clearing for a moment. "What are you talking about?"

"Let me take ye away. It's too dangerous for you to stay." Thomas nodded to the letter. "We should leave now."

Her lips parted and her gaze flashed angrily. "I will not run away."

"A man is dead, Lottie!" Thomas shook her shoulders. "And now someone is trying to blackmail ye. I shall not stand by and watch while ye are in danger."

She pushed his hands away. "You have no right to decide when I go or stay. If I leave now, it will only prove my guilt to Mr. de Lacy. What if he uses that as an excuse to investigate what we did to his brother?" Her voice broke and her head bowed. "Do you truly think that I would leave and let my pregnant sister suffer the consequences?"

Thomas sighed, pressing the palms of his hands against his temples. He didn't know the full story of what happened to Edmund, but he knew that William and Fidelia were directly responsible. He had seen Edmund's body that night on the beach, and the reminder of the incident had caused Fidelia to collapse from shock.

"Of course not," Thomas said quietly. The accusations, coupled with the note, were making him mad with worry for her. What if Thomas couldn't protect her this time? Impulsively, he wrapped an arm around her and pulled her in a gentle hug. "I was not suggesting that ye abandon yer family. I... I just cannot bear the thought of something happening to ye again."

Lottie tensed in shock, but slowly, she relaxed and laid her head against his shoulder. "The only way to ensure that Mr. de Lacy cannot arrest me for the murder or dig further into our past with Edmund is to reveal Mr. Farraday's real killer," Lottie said.

Thomas rested his chin on her head, savoring the comfort of holding her in his arms. For the moment, he could convince himself that if she were by his side, he could keep her safe. If anyone saw them, it would ruin Lottie's reputation and quite possibly get him drawn and quartered, but neither of them pulled away.

"How do we do that?" Thomas asked finally, closing his eyes with resignation. If he couldn't take Lottie far away, then he would stand by her side and help prove her innocence, no matter the consequences.

"The guests," Lottie said, pulling back to look at him. "When I burned the papers, Mr. Farraday mentioned an associate hidden among the guests... someone I would never suspect."

***Lottie stared at the guests across from her at the breakfast table the next morning, her fork paused halfway to her mouth.

Their mood was still light, but the surprise addition of Mr. de Lacy to the house party had caused quite a stir. Lady Harrington and her son seemed amiable to him, and Mrs. Ashdown seemed eager to test his worthiness as a potential suitor to her niece, Miss Wilde. The younger woman, for her part, had avoided him once she learned he was the local magistrate. Perhaps such a position was too low for her, Lottie thought, eyeing the mousy girl sideways. Or was it that Mr. Farraday's accomplice was a woman...?

"Miss Wilde thinks he's too old for her," Catriona's cheerful whisper made Lottie jump and fumble with her fork.

"Merciful heavens, Catriona!" Lottie gasped, a hand flying to her throat as she tried to calm her nervous heart. The young woman was as quiet and frightening as a ghost.

Catriona shrugged with a slow smile, and Lottie remembered Octavia's gossip that the younger half-sister of Lord Campbell was the daughter of a witch. "I was just telling you that she's no competition, if that was what you were wondering about."

Lottie raised an eyebrow. For once, Catriona's intuition was wrong. "I have no interest in Mr. de Lacy, believe me," she shoveled a forkful of breakfast into her mouth and chewed with vigor. Even the thought of that man still made her blood boil, purely for the fact that he was related to Edmund.

"Oh, I believe you," Catriona said with a knowing wink. "You have eyes for a different set of broad shoulders..."

Lottie's neck flushed and her eyes darted to the door. Thomas hadn't arrived yet since he was still serving William and Fidelia that morning. "You—" Lottie broke off and force her voice to lower. "How do you know that?"

Catriona giggled. "Oh, I have my ways. But be careful. That young man you fancy isn't who he says he is."

"What do you mean?" Lottie asked, her gaze circling the room. Everyone else was engaged in conversation, but Mr. de Lacy watched her as he listened to Sir Roland ramble on.

Catriona tapped the side of her nose conspiratorily and sighed. "Anyway, that's too boring to talk about so early in the morning. Now, that Mr. de Lacy on the other hand... he's rather handsome, isn't he? Even if he is ancient enough to have one foot in the grave."

Lottie cringed. Yes, he was handsome all right... just like Edmund. But he was hardly ancient, perhaps in his early thirties. But to the young and impulsive Catriona, he must seem as old and boring as a man in his sixties.

"What are you girls discussing so secretively?" Mrs. Ashdown asked, coming to sit on Lottie's other side and leaning into the conversation. She was a woman who may have once been considered a beauty, with light blond hair more silver than yellow, and a pleasant face heavily weighed down with makeup.

"Mr. de Lacy," Catriona said, nodding towards the man in question. "He is handsome enough but comes from a poor family and is entirely too old for us. And he looks rather frightening in his hat and cloak."

Lottie paused, staring at Catriona. Hat and cloak...? When had she seen him dressed like that?

Mrs. Ashdown nodded in agreement with Catriona's pronouncement upon Mr. de Lacy. "His eyes seem to peer right through you to the bone, don't they?" she whispered with a giggle. "Luckily, my darling niece has better options than that," Mrs. Ashdown looked across the room to where all the men had gathered to discuss politics.

"Oh?" Catriona asked, following her gaze. "Have you secured a marriage for her already?"

Mrs. Ashdown's eyes danced, but Lottie thought they looked more greedy than happy. "Oh, let us just say that I have seen something quite valuable. With it, I shall secure my young niece's future—and my own, since she shall take care of me in my old age," Mrs. Ashdown laughed.

Catriona laughed along politely, but Lottie furrowed her brow. What could Mrs. Ashdown have seen that made her so confident?

Before she could ask, however, the door opened. William entered, followed by Thomas. Dark circles stood out under the former's eyes and he looked exhausted and worried. Thomas's gaze sought Lottie's and his lips twitched in a tired smile at the sight of her.

Lottie excused herself from the conversation as fast as she could and sat near William at the head of the table. He rubbed his brow wearily as a servant set a plate in front of him, but he ignored the food. Thomas pushed Lottie's chair in and stepped back to join the other servants.

"How is Fidelia?" Lottie whispered, leaning forward to block Mr. de Lacy's view of William.

William sighed and winced. "She is alright now. The doctor said that the shock caused pre-term contractions, but they have eased, finally. She is sleeping."

Lottie's shoulders sagged with relief. "That is good news. And the child?"

"I... The doctor says everything seems to be back to normal, but we will know more in a few days if... if..." William's voice trailed off and his eyes grew unfocused.

Lottie grasped his hand tightly. "Everything will be fine, I promise," she said with a wane smile. "And do not worry about Mr. de Lacy, Thomas and I will take care of him. Just be there for Fidelia."

William nodded and patted her hand with his other one, but Lottie was not sure if he had heard her.

After a while, Lottie finally convinced him to eat, and she decided she needed something to take her mind off everything so she could approach her investigation with a clear head. Fidelia and William needed her, and Lottie was determined not to fail them.

***

Later that afternoon, Lottie leaned over one of her worktables in her laboratory, examining a small pile of black powder. With all the excitement from the past few days, she had not had a chance to experiment with it yet. Now that Puppy, her pet cat, was safely locked away in her room, she was ready for her first test.

"With that amount, ye'll likely blow yer hand off, wee Lassie," Thomas said from the doorway.

Lottie jumped, the lit matchstick in her fingers flying from her fingers and landing dangerously close to her box of fireworks. She gasped, but Thomas quickly stamped it out before it could catch the rug on fire.

"What are you doing here?" Lottie asked as she straightened and dusted off her apron.

"Checking on ye," Thomas said with a grin. "I see I was right to. Do ye know what ye are doing with that?" he gestured to the pile of black powder.

"I have loaded and fired guns before," Lottie said hesitantly, "But I've... never dealt with this much quantity of powder. I am trying to recreate the blast of a firework, you see."

Thomas joined her at the table and leaned closure, squinting at the pile. "The black powder in fireworks is mixed with other materials to create specific blast sizes and colors. Ye will blow yerself up before ye recreate it simply by adding more black powder."

"I am a scientist," Lottie said, rolling her eyes and striking another match. "Half of the fun is in dangerously experimenting."

"Wait--!" Thomas shouted, pulling her backward. But it was too late, Lottie had already flicked the match towards the small pile.

CRACK!

Light flashed in Lottie's face, following immediately by a wave of thick white smoke as she fell back atop Thomas.

***

Eyebrows on a Potato

Thomas grunted as Lottie's elbow dug into his ribs when they landed on the rug. Thick white smoke swirled around them as Lottie groaned, her hair tickling his chin.

Lottie rolled off his chest, which had cushioned her fall, and Thomas sucked in a breath and immediately coughed. "Are ye mad, woman?" he waved an arm through the air to clear the smoke.

Stunned, Lottie slowly began to giggle. "Marvelous," she said, staring at the blast mark on the table.

The smoke finally cleared out the open door and Thomas muttered under his breath, sitting up. "Ye truly shall be the death of me-" he glanced at Lottie and squawked. He slapped his hand over his mouth to stop the sound, but his lips were already beginning to twitch with laughter.

"What?" Lottie said, eyes widening. She touched her cheeks, smearing black soot over her lovely face.

"Saints alive!" Thomas's laughter finally broke free. "Yer eyebrows, Lassie! Ye've blown yer eyebrows clean off!"

Not only that, but her golden hair, now grey with smoke, was singed. The tips of the baby-fine strands that framed her face were curled and browned.

Lottie gasped, feeling for what was left of her eyebrows. She squealed and slapped her hands over the bare spots. "Don't look!"

Thomas roared with laughter, falling back onto the rug, holding his sides.

"Ugh! You-how could you laugh at me?" Lottie smacked his chest, but he only laughed harder, snatching her hand. He tugged and she landed on him, her face coming dangerously close to his.

Thomas hugged her tightly as his chortles faded. "Thank goodness ye weren't hurt," he grinned, shaking his head.

Lottie's lips turned down in a pretty pout and Thomas's gaze paused on them for too long.

His breathing hitched. "Lottie... I-"

"Thank you for pulling me back," Lottie said, her lashes fluttering as she sat up, sliding from his arms.

Thomas blinked, wishing he were better with words. Perhaps then he could express the feelings that were becoming all-consuming in his mind and heart. But now was not the time, he reminded himself as he sat up.

Lottie retrieved a small hand-held mirror from her writing desk. She squealed again at her reflection and slapped it back onto the desk. "Oh, humdudgeon!" she swore, covering her missing eyebrows again.

Thomas stood and took her hand gently. "T'is not all bad," he said, pursing his lips to hide his grin.

"I look like a potato!" Lottie wailed.

"A pretty potato," Thomas bumped Lottie under the chin with a knuckle. "Prettiest I've ever seen, and I've eaten my fair share, so that should say something. Besides, it was a rather exciting experiment!"

Rolling her eyes, Lottie sighed even as she smiled. "You are the only one in the entire world who could make me laugh after burning my eyebrows to kingdom-come."

"Then I have earned my wages for today, I'd say," he said, rubbing his thumb absent-mindedly over her fingers. "Motivation to keep me around, aye?"

"But what am I going to do?" Lottie's voice broke as she covered her face with her other hand. "I can not leave the room looking like this. What if the guests see?"

Thomas chewed his lip and eyed the rug behind them. "Hmm... I might have an idea."

***

Thomas whistled innocently, shrugging the rolled-up rug higher onto his shoulder.

Lottie grunted from inside and Thomas fought back another smile.

"Why I ever let you talk me into this..." Lottie muttered, but Thomas could still hear her.

"T'is my revenge for almost blowing me up," Thomas replied.

Just then, Octavia Palmer rounded the corner, a note clutched in her hand. Thomas slowed, tightening his hold around Lottie's legs inside the rug. The long corridor had no doors; they would have to pass each other.

Octavia didn't look up until she almost ran into him. She blinked in surprise, backing up a step. "Oh, pardon me," she said politely, even though he was dressed as a footman.

Thomas dipped his head and averted his gaze. He tried to edge around her, but she stepped in front of him again.

"Are you Mr. Hawthorne, Lottie's friend?" Octavia asked, her brows pinched together with worry.

"Aye, Miss," Thomas said hesitantly.

"I must speak with her. It's urgent," Octavia shifted nervously and looked around. "Do you know where she is?"

"Ahh," Thomas glanced at the rug and Lottie shifted inside like she was trying to shrink down more. "Nay, Miss. I have nay seen her for a wee while."

"Oh," Octavia's shoulders slumped. Then she glanced at the rug and arched a brow. "What are you doing with that?"

Thomas opened his mouth and paused. "Rats... rat infestation. Aye."

"It's... breathing," Octavia stepped closer.

"Very big rats," he smacked the rug, realizing too late that it was the spot over Lottie's rump. She jerked and he winced with mortification. She would never forgive him for that, he was sure.

Octavia cringed and stepped back. "Please tell Lottie that I'm looking for her," she said and hurried down the hall.

Lottie muttered angrily inside the rug but Thomas only grinned and walked faster towards her room. Thankfully, the hallway around her room was empty and he didn't pass anyone else on his way.

Once safely inside, he laid the rug down gently and gave it a push.

Lottie rolled out, looking even more disheveled as her already-singed hair crackled with static electricity. Her cheeks, still smeared with soot, looked red. "If you smacked my bottom, I shall remove your hand from your body."

Thomas gulped. He grinned awkwardly and held up the offending hand. "It... was an accident, I swear."

Lottie glared at him for a moment before she sighed and stood, dusting off her rumpled skirts. She faced the large oval mirror over her toiletry table. With a sigh, she wiped at the soot, pausing over her missing eyebrows. "I look rather hopeless, don't I? Thank goodness I am not trying to catch myself a husband."

The statement made Thomas feel both relieved... and slightly disappointed. He joined her and gestured for her to sit on the chair. He poured fresh water into the basin and dipped a washcloth in and he gently wiped the soot from her face. Even without eyebrows, she was lovely.

Lottie giggled as he playfully wiped at her ears and he grinned. "Aye, there she is," he said, leaning back against the table to admire his work. "Pretty as ever."

"For a potato, you mean," Lottie teased.

Thomas nodded seriously and she laughed, shoving him gently. But then her smile faded as she examined herself in the mirror. Now that the soot was gone, the absence of her eyebrows was even more glaring. "Whatever shall I do?" Lottie moaned, covering the spaces again.

With a small smile, Thomas searched through her makeup until he found the powder Sally used to darken Lottie's light brown eyebrows. "May I?" he asked, holding up one of her thin brushes.

"It couldn't look worse than it already is," Lottie sighed, waving him on.

Thomas mixed a bit of water with the powder and leaned close enough that he could feel her breath on his cheeks as he carefully painted.

"How do you know so much about a lady's makeup?" Lottie asked, narrowing her eyes with teasing suspicion.

"Hush," Thomas chided gently. "This is art, after all."

Lottie smiled and closed her eyes obediently.

Thomas paused, memorizing the curve of her cheeks, the pretty lashes that rest against them... and those rosebud lips. Shaking his head to clear it, he continued painting. "As a boy, I used to watch my mother paint her eyebrows to darken them. She was a rather free-spirited woman, and she would tell me the most fantastical stories as she got ready."

"You've never mentioned your family before," Lottie mumbled, trying not to move her face.

Thomas's hand stilled for a moment. "They're dead. Or rather, I am dead to those who still live. My mother passed not long after my sister was born, the rest disowned me when I came back alive from the war."

"Oh," Lottie said.

"There," Thomas said with slight pride. He had managed to mimic individual hairs so that it wasn't a thick line of paint, but it would still be obvious to those standing close.

Lottie examined herself in the mirror and nodded thoughtfully. "I am impressed, Mr. Hawthorne."

"Thank ye, thank ye," he bowed mockingly.

Lottie clucked her tongue and eyed him sideways. "Sadly, I've always been rubbish with painting. I doubt Sally has ever had to paint such fine strokes, either."

With a grin, Thomas tapped the tip of her nose. "Very well, wee Lassie, I shall do yer makeup any time ye desire."

"It's a life-long job," Lottie warned playfully. "Who knows if they will ever grow back!"

Thomas's heart constricted and his smile slipped as he stared at her. "Aye. If ye wish it, I shall remain by yer side for the rest of my days."

Lottie jumped to her feet and hugged him.

Coughing awkwardly, Thomas hugged her back for only a moment. "Come, now," he said and pulled away. "I should leave. T'wouldn't be proper for me to stay longer."

Lottie reddened as if suddenly realizing that she was alone with a man in her room. She quickly shooed him out, but Thomas paused in the hallway after she closed the door. Holding his hand over his pounding heart, he leaned his back against the door.

"For all my days," he whispered again.

Ripped Seams and Bloody Boots

A fter Lottie bathed, careful not to smear the makeup that Thomas had painted in place of her burned-off eyebrows, she snipped the ends of her burnt hair with a pair of scissors. With the browned, curled ends gone, she could almost believe that her experiment hadn't gone horribly wrong. Almost.

Sally arrived soon after to help her dress for dinner. "Miss, the seamstress sent a letter asking about your dress for the Christmas Masquerade ball—Oh my."

Lottie winced, discretely covering her eyebrows as best she could. "I know, I know," she groaned.

Sally shook her head, eyes wide with innocence. "I don't know what you're talking about, Miss."

Lottie sighed and gestured for the note. "Oh well, perhaps the guests won't be as observant. What does the letter say?"

Taking her place behind Lottie to style her hair, Sally took up a brush. "She believes she has found a costume that will suit you and wants to come tomorrow for a final fitting."

Lottie nodded absently, her thoughts drifting to Thomas. Would he be there at the ball as a footman? It would be so much easier if she could dance with him instead, but it would never be allowed. After all, he was just a servant, and Lottie was the charge of the Earl and Countess of Durham.

***Checking her hair one last time for any burned ends that she might have missed, Lottie joined the Earl and Countess beside the door to the dining room. Their heads were bent together, deep in discussion about preparations for their new grandchild, and Lottie smiled at the sight. The Countess had been quite difficult when the Atwell sisters first arrived in England, but behind her fierce countenance was a soft, loving woman who truly doted on Lottie and Fidelia.

William's cane clicked in the hallway and Lottie turned, brightening to see Fidelia sitting in the wheeled chair, pushed by Thomas.

"Fidelia!" Lottie ran to kiss her sister's cheek. She looked more tired and pale, but her green eyes were bright as ever.

"Devil's beard!" William squawked and Lottie cringed. "What happened to your eyebrows?"

Lottie sputtered, pointing to her face, and then towards her laboratory. Finally, she shrugged and looked to Thomas for help. All eyes turned to him.

Thomas held up his hands and imitated an explosion with his fingers. "Ka-boom!"

William nodded slowly, his lips parted in a cringe. "Ah-hah..."

Fidelia giggled, patting Lottie on the hand. "You will likely kill that man one of these days," she whispered.

"So he tells me. Daily," Lottie muttered, taking the wheeled chair from Thomas.

Behind her, Thomas leaned close to William and whispered, "I do believe Miss Lottie is certifiably insane."

William chuckled, "It's genetic, my friend. Entirely genetic."

Lottie and Fidelia both whipped around to glare at the men.

Thomas and William gulped simultaneously. They were saved by the arrival of the other guests, and Lottie quickly busied herself with helping Fidelia so no one else could comment on her missing eyebrows.

At supper, Lottie found herself seated with Octavia on one side, and Mrs. Ashdown on the other. Sir Roland and Mr. de Lacy sat across from them, engrossed in conversation with Lord Campbell.

"When should we expect an announcement of your wedding?" Mrs. Ashdown asked suddenly.

Lottie choked on her soup. Octavia patted her on the back gently, and Thomas, from his position with the other footman across the room, stepped forward as if to come to Lottie's aid.

She shook her head minutely and glanced at him over her napkin as she coughed into delicately.

Thomas's hands clenched, but he stepped back into line, his eyes never leaving hers.

"I beg your pardon?" Lottie asked Mrs. Ashdown, sipping some of her wine a little too quickly.

"A woman of eighteen such as yourself should be married by now," Mrs. Ashdown said, turning her nose up a little as she sniffed. "And with the dowery that the Earl has so graciously provided you, I'm sure you have no shortage of suitors."

Lottie thought she saw Thomas tense across the room behind the row of chairs.

"Yes," Mr. de Lacy broke into the conversation from across the table. "Why haven't you married? Was there perhaps a scandal?" His eyes darkened and Lottie wondered if he was hinting something about Edmund.

Could Mr. Farraday have written anything else about what he knew of Lottie's secrets? But Mr. Farraday had never mentioned Edmund.

"I have yet to receive any marriage proposals this season," Lottie said, glaring at Mr. de Lacy.

Mrs. Ashdown clucked her tongue. "There's always next season. Now, my darling niece, on the other hand..."

Lottie tuned out Mrs. Ashdown's sprawling, and repetitive account of Miss Wilde's many virtues, which were sure to land her a wealthy husband, and she stared at Mr. de Lacy. He studied her closely, but his eyes were more curious now than suspicious.

Mrs. Ashdown leaned closer, pushing a letter into Lottie's face. "See, just look at this wonderful handwriting!"

Grateful for the distraction, Lottie smiled at Mrs. Ashdown and examined the well-worn letter with her. She must have treasured it dearly, for it had been folded and unfolded enough times that holes were wearing their way through the creases. The ink was smeared slightly as if the writer's hand and wrist had passed over it as she wrote quickly. Lottie had seen that with left-handed writers before, but it was not very common.

"My niece wrote me every month while she was in the Caribbean on her uncle's plantation," Mrs. Ashdown explained fondly. Miss Wilde tensed from across the table, her face paling when she saw the letter. "But this was the last one she sent before she boarded the ship back to see me. See how lovely her handwriting is? And look at how attentive she was to the details of the flowers and animals..."

Lottie nodded politely. The letter looked rather boring, but at least it kept the conversation off her marriage prospects.

On her other side, Octavia leaned closer to see the letter. A tiny rip sounded from her dress and she froze. Lottie glanced down quickly as Octavia sat statue-still.

"How bad is it?" Octavia muttered from the corner of her mouth.

Lottie cringed. "Bad, I'm afraid." The threads along the seam of her empire waist were quickly unraveling. At this rate, the top of her dress would separate from the bottom entirely in a matter of minutes!

Octavia straightened her shoulders like a captain resigned to go down with the ship. "Well, I suppose it worked out for Lady Godiva..." she grinned.

"I suddenly feel quite ill," Lottie announced to the table. "I beg your pardon," she looked at William near the head of the table and winked. He raised his brows but waved his hand. The men at the table stood and bowed slightly.

"Won't you help me, dear Octavia?" Lottie asked, grabbing a handful of Octavia's skirt to keep it from tearing more as her friend stood.

Thomas stepped forward to help, but Lottie flicked her hand behind her to wave him off. Keeping herself between the rest of the room and Octavia, they scurried from the room.

Octavia laughed ruefully as they hurried down the hallway, holding her dress together as the rest of the threads unraveled completely. "Just my luck. Do you think Captain Hillington saw?"

"If he did, you could use it to entrap him in a marriage," Lottie teased and they finally reached Octavia's room, just a few doors down from Lottie's.

Safely inside, Lottie helped Octavia out of the ruined dress. "Octavia, these stitches..." Lottie examined the unraveled waistline. "Whoever sewed this did a rubbish job."

Octavia reddened and she quickly took the dress from Lottie's hand. "It's—Nevermind that. Can you fetch me another one?"

Lottie chewed her lip, confused by her friend's sudden roughness, but opened the wardrobe to sort through the dresses. The first one was also pulling apart at the seams, and the next two weren't fitting for dinnertime. A piece of paper stuck out of the most suitable dress, and Lottie fished it out as she pulled the dress down.

"Why are you so fixed on Captain Hillington, anyway? He seems rather... boring if you don't mind me saying. You act proper and refined, but I know you well enough to see that you need someone more adventurous," Lottie said absently as she unfolded the note.

Octavia sighed and Lottie could hear her drop heavily onto the bed. "He's rich. And no matter how much I would like adventure, I need the money more."

I know what you're hiding, Miss Palmer, the note read, and Lottie's hands began to shake as she read on. With a sinking feeling, she recognized the handwriting. Meet me on the castle roof tonight, or I shall ruin your father forever.

The note slipped from Lottie's fingers, landing with a rustle in the bottom of the wardrobe.

Bending slowly, Lottie reached for the note. It had to be a mistake. She must a read it wrong.

But what if it wasn't? Hadn't Mr. Farraday handed Octavia a note that night before he was killed? What was it she had said?

"I'll make him pay..." Octavia's words from that night flitted through Lottie's mind.

As she found the note, her eyes fell on a pair of Octavia's boots, pushed into the darkest corner of the wardrobe. But even in the shadows, Lottie could see the blood encrusting the bottom inch of the leather.

Bloody grains of sand were scattered around the boots.

Lottie dropped the dress and turned, withdrawing the boots and note.

"Octavia... why did you kill Mr. Farraday?"

Octavia's Secret

T homas watched Lottie leave; his hands balled into fists. Watching Mr. de Lacy so blatantly target her made him itch under the collar, and it couldn't be a coincidence that she left so quickly after he hinted something about Edmund.

Thomas listened closely to the dinner conversations from his place in line with the other footmen as the meal progressed.

"Is it not strange that Mr. Farraday left so suddenly?" Miss Catriona said, looking around the table with keen, dark eyes.

"If you ask me," Sir Rolland sputtered, "it's no loss to our party that Mr. Farraday has left. He was nothing but trouble."

Lady Hillington nodded, her neck reddening. "Indeed. What an odious, nosy man."

"I didn't think he was so bad," her son, Captain Hillington, shrugged, but his eyes flashed and Thomas wondered if his response was a lie.

Mr. de Lacy must have seen it too, for he leaned forward casually. "Who was Mr. Farraday?"

Captain Hillington paused, setting his fork down slowly. "Just another guest who left yesterday morning."

"Did you happen to see him off?" Mr. de Lacy rubbed his thumb slowly across the rim of his wine glass.

"I did, just before dawn," Lord Campbell interjected. "Although he ignored me when I greeted him. In a terrible hurry, he was. Mr. Farraday was normally rather cordial, but he had his hat pulled low over his face and the collar of his cloak up. Rather rubbish, I must say."

Thomas started, his head cocking slightly at Lord Campbell's account of seeing Mr. Farraday leave. Whoever Lord Campbell had seen, it couldn't have been Mr. Farraday. Thomas knew beyond a doubt that he was already dead before dawn.

"How mysterious," Mr. de Lacy murmured and his thumb paused.

As dinner drew to a close and Lottie still hadn't returned with Octavia, the Countess announced that they would all retire to the drawing room. Lord Campbell suggested they play a round of cards, but Mrs. Ashdown argued that her niece, Miss Wilde, should play the pianoforte for them all. The poor girl looked stricken at the idea.

As the guests filed out to the drawing room, Mr. de Lacy hung back, pretending to examine the crown molding of the dining room.

"A word, Mr. Hawthorne?" Mr. de Lacy said, clasping his hands behind his back, his head still tipped back to look at the ceiling.

Thomas looked at the other footmen, who had gone to assist the guests, and hesitated. He wasn't sure he could control his temper if he were left alone with the man who was tormenting Lottie.

"Aye, sir?" Thomas said finally, joining his side.

"Did you notice anything strange about that conversation?" Mr. de Lacy asked quietly, but his tone was still light.

Thomas tugged at the hem of his gilded sleeve thoughtfully. "Aye, sir. They all spoke about Mr. Farraday in the past tense... as if they all knew he was already dead."

Mr. de Lacy nodded, a smile twitching at his lips. "Precisely."

*** Lottie held the boot up higher and advanced as Octavia sat up slowly on her bed.

"What are you doing with those?" Octavia whispered, her face pale.

"You killed Mr. Farraday," Lottie stated, her throat tight as she confronted her friend. "Why?"

Octavia shook her head and her face darkened. "I didn't kill him."

"Then why are your boot covered in blood and sand? The killer moved his body from the beach, dragging him into the water," Lottie's hand began to shake.

"This is madness, Lottie. I swear I never harmed him! I couldn't have been the one to drag his body into the water; the blood and sand would have washed away," Octavia said as she rose to her feet. She moved slowly, like a cornered cat.

Lottie blinked, looking away for a moment as she thought it through. Octavia seized the chance and snatched the note from Lottie's other hand.

Her apparent calmness gone, Octavia drew a shaking breath and crumpled the note in her fist. "Did you read it?"

Lottie nodded and tried to push away her guilt. Octavia was right, of course, if she had been the one to drag Mr. Farraday into the water, she wouldn't still have blood and sand on her boots.

Octavia whimpered, clutching at the roots of her glossy, mahogany curls. "Oh, what am I going to do?" she whispered. "Please, please, believe me, Lottie. I was desperate, but I did not kill him."

"I... I believe you," Lottie said, her voice catching. Was she being too trusting since Octavia was her friend? "But...What did Mr. Farraday mean in that letter?"

Octavia chuckled, a harsh, rueful sound and she sat back down on her bed. Even in her distressed state, her shoulders remained ramrod straight. She had the quiet confidence of a captain's daughter, and anyone could see it in her bearing. "Somehow, Mr. Farraday found out about my family's darkest secret. He was going to ruin me. Ruin everything. My father would die if I didn't give in to his demands."

Lottie's gaze flicked to the bottom half of Octavia's dress, which was now crumpled on the floor. "The stitches... you did them, didn't you?" she asked, slowly piecing things together. The clothes from last season... no new gowns... Octavia's desperation to snare the wealthy Captain Hillington. "The only reason you would fix the dress yourself is if... You're destitute, aren't you?"

Octavia smiled and shook her head as she stared at the wall. "Entirely. We are living on the remnants of my dowery. I have sold everything else that we can and have hidden my parents away in a tiny cottage, telling everyone in the ton that they are ill and visiting family in the north."

"I don't understand," Lottie sat next to her friend, touching her arm comfortingly. "Your father is well known for being a wealthy merchant."

"That was before Britain and America went to war again," Octavia explained. "My father had taken a very risky venture to the Orient. Very few ships are allowed in China, you see, and no one had yet secured an official trade agreement. My father has traded with them for decades and promised his investors that he could secure an actual agreement and a massive return."

"That was when I met you on the boat leaving Baltimore?" Lottie asked, trying to remember that chaotic time. She had still been reeling from her first escape from Le Coquin. Hadn't Octavia said her father had lost something very precious?

Octavia sighed, and she nodded in resignation. "We had docked in Baltimore to restock supplies before traveling across the Atlantic. When America declared war, their navy confiscated our boat... and the trade agreement with China. It was hidden in a secret compartment in my father's cabin, but I couldn't retrieve it before we had to abandon ship. We barely escaped with our lives, but... the investors still needed to be paid."

"Oh," Lottie breathed. "Thus, you've been paying them this whole time, pretending that everything is alright, and their investment is secure?"

For the first time, Octavia's shoulders slumped, and she buried her face in her hands. "My father borrowed so much money from them to fund the venture. If I do not pay them monthly, they will get suspicious. If they know the truth, my father will be sent to the debtor's prison. His health has been so poor... he wouldn't survive a day in there."

Lottie stood, tapping her fingers against the boots as she thought. "Mr. Farraday said he lost a large investment and needed to gather funds quickly... he was one of your father's investors, wasn't he? He found out that the trade agreement was lost and tried to blackmail you to cover the difference. But what could he have wanted? Surely you have nothing left of value?"

"I never found out. I think he was already dead by the time I went to meet him," Octavia gestured to the bloody boots. "Mr. Farraday told me to meet him on the castle rooftop that night, but the only way that I knew how to get there was the spiral staircase leading up to your laboratory. When he wasn't on the roof, I went to search... and I found him. Or rather, what had happened to him."

"Where?" Lottie held the boots out to Octavia, who took them with a grimace. "What did you find?"

"You had better come with me."

After Octavia dressed, she led Lottie out into the castle and up the spiral staircase to Lottie's laboratory.

"I don't understand," Lottie said, shaking her head as they entered her disheveled workspace. It still smelled slightly of black powder, but at least the smoke was entirely gone. "You found Mr. Farraday in here?"

Octavia bit her lip and twisted her hands together. "His body was already gone. But... I did not mean to cover it up. Truly... but I was so panicked that I thought you... I thought you had done it."

Lottie watched with a sinking feeling as Octavia strode to the far side of the room, where the remnants of Lottie's clock system lay scattered about. In her haste to start experimenting with the black powder, she had not noticed that the spear holding the cogs in place was missing.

Octavia pulled back one of the many rugs that adorned the cold stone floor, revealing a large pool of dried blood.

Mr. Farraday had been killed in Lottie's laboratory.

***Hi guys! What did you think of Octavia's secret? Psst... it's leading into book 3... which has pirates... but you didn't hear that from me ;)

If you liked this chapter, please be sure to vote and comment!

Worried About You

"What hour were you supposed to meet with Mr. Farraday?" Lottie asked, staring at the dried pool of blood. It looked like Octavia had tried unsuccessfully to clean it, but the stain was still evident.

"He did not give me a time," Octavia said, laying the rug back over the blood and rubbed her hands together as if trying to erase the memory. Blood from the wound that Lottie had caused on her hand was beginning to darken her bandage as if she had reopened the gash with the stress.

Octavia continued, "he just said that he would be there when I looked for him. I did try to meet with him around midnight, but he was not there, even after I waited for an hour."

"Because he was meeting with me. Here, at the laboratory." Lottie turned toward the fire and chewed on her thumbnail, her mind churning. "What about when you found the blood? It had to be rather fresh if it could stain your boots."

Pursing her lips thoughtfully, Octavia tipped her head. "It was in the early morning hours after I woke up to hear you screaming. You left and then Sally patched up my hand, and I went to find him. I thought that maybe he was the one causing your nightmares... and then I found the blood... I truly thought you must have killed him in your crazed state."

"I left him sometime between 1:30 and 2:00," Lottie said, nodding slowly. "And you found the blood around 6:00. If my spear is missing, it must have been used to kill him, either accidentally or intentionally. But I have no knowledge about how long this much blood would take to dry—"

"This much? Without sunlight, it could take several hours to get to the state in which I found it," Octavia said with confidence. Lottie turned a wide-eyed stare to her, and Octavia grinned. "I have seen my fair share of skirmishes aboard my father's ships, remember?"

Lottie grimaced, unsure if she should be impressed or concerned. "Then he could have died anytime between when I left him, and you found the blood. I fear that does not make things much easier for us."

Octavia nodded. "Oh, there's more," she walked backward to the door, pointing to an imaginary line on the floor. "There was a trail of it leading out of the room, but I managed to clean it up."

"Where did it go?" Lottie asked eagerly. Perhaps she could follow the trail and find some hint about who moved the body before Octavia arrived.

Octavia led the way down several stairs and to the door that led to the roof. "It was the trail that I discovered first. It led me up to your laboratory. But there was nothing on the roof to say where the body went. I am not sure how someone could have gotten it out of the castle without anyone noticing."

With her stomach twisting, Lottie stepped closer to the edge of the roof. "I think I know." She looked over the edge. Her pully system dangled not far below, red stains on the ropes and netting.

"My inventions. One was used to kill Mr. Farraday... and the other was used to move him. I never imagined they could be put to such horrific purposes," Lottie whispered, shaking her head.

Octavia put a comforting arm around Lottie's shoulders.

Lottie sighed, but then she looked up at Octavia quickly. "The bloody sand. If you did not know where the body had gone, then you never followed it to the beach. How could there be bloody sand in your wardrobe?"

*** Thomas followed Mr. de Lacy to the drawing-room as he joined the rest of the guests, who were just starting a round of cribbage.

Taking his place behind William's chair, he watched Mr. de Lacy slowly circle the room before choosing a seat far enough back to view the entire group of players, but close enough that he could still hear the conversation.

Sir Roland eyed his cards and grunted, his ears reddening. "Don't forget the money you still owe me from our last bet, Campbell," he winked at Lord Campbell.

Lord Campbell rolled his eyes but smiled stiffly. "Of course not, Sir Roland. I can pay at any time, but let's see if I can't win it back this round, eh?"

Finally looking at ease, Miss Wilde confidently placed her bet as she held her cards coquettishly to her nose.

Thomas had never been a gambling man, but he paid close attention as the game and conversation progressed, looking for any more signs that one of the guests was hiding something.

The door creaked as Lottie and Octavia returned, both looking rather pale. Thomas's heart tightened, but he forced himself to remain in his place behind William. Lottie paused to meet Thomas's gaze and she drew in a slow breath as if steadying herself.

Lottie's eyes turned to Fidelia, who had slumped over slightly in her wheeled chair, and her face softened. She knelt beside Fidelia and touched her hand gently.

"Charles?" Fidelia mumbled, her lashes fluttering sleepily.

Lottie's brows pinched and she looked to William, who shook his head slightly. Lottie sighed, forcing a small smile. "No, dearest, it's just me."

"Oh," Fidelia's face fell, and she sat up straighter. "I must have been dreaming. I thought... I thought he was here."

William frowned and stood to excused himself and his wife. Lottie glanced up at Thomas and quickly offered to walk them back to their rooms.

As William pushed the wheeled chair along the hallway several steps ahead, Fidelia already asleep again, Thomas fell into step beside Lottie.

"What happened? Where have ye been?" Thomas asked, nudging Lottie's hand.

"I just accused my dearest friend of murder," Lottie said, and she seemed a bit stunned.

"What?" Thomas gasped, grabbing her arm to turn her to face him. "Do you realize how dangerous that was?"

Lottie blinked, pulling her head back slightly as if surprised by his fierce response. "How could I have been in any danger?"

Thomas's shoulders fell in exasperation. "This is murder, Lottie! If the murderer knows that ye suspect them, ye will get yerself killed!"

Her face paled again as if the thought had never occurred to her, and she stared at him. "But... Octavia is innocent."

"This time," Thomas shook his head, pulling her into a tight embrace as relief washed over him. She could have been killed, and he had had no idea she was even in danger. "This time ye were lucky. But promise me that ye will no' go wandering off with someone like that again. I cannot protect ye if I am no' there."

Lottie paused, and she hesitantly leaned her cheek against his chest. "I didn't realize you were so worried for me."

I worry about ye every moment of the day, Thomas thought silently, tightening his arms around her waist.

William coughed ahead of them and they both broke apart, cheeks burning. William had turned to look over his shoulder, a bemused smile playing at his lips. "Are you quite finished?"

Lottie reddened and hurried ahead of Thomas.

He looked after her, wishing he had the right to hold her. If he did, he would never let her go.

*** Once Lottie helped William get Fidelia settled into their bed, she and Thomas quickly excused themselves and walked slowly back to the drawing-room. In a low voice, Lottie explained Octavia's revelations and her discovery that her pully system had been used to move the body out of the castle.

Thomas stiffened beside her and his step slowed. "Perhaps we should leave things be, Lassie," he said, and his hand brushed against hers.

Tingles raced up Lottie's arm and traveled pleasantly down her spine, but she ignored them. "Whoever murdered Mr. Farraday is still trying to blackmail me," she shook her head firmly. "William and Fidelia will only be safe when I stop them. I cannot give up now."

"What if the killer and the blackmailer are different people?" Thomas shifted his weight.

Lottie shook her head. "Somehow, I feel they must be one and the same. Mr. Farraday said his partner was here. Maybe the partner got tired of working under Mr. Farraday and realized they could reap the fruits of their blackmail without Mr. Farraday since they also had knowledge of their victims' secrets. Either way, the partner is the most suspicious person."

"What will ye do when ye find the killer?" Thomas asked quietly, his eyes not meeting hers.

Lottie thought for a moment, taking a deep breath. "I have to stop them... whatever the cost. Even if it means I must kill them, I will protect my family."

Thomas was silent the rest of the way to the drawing-room. Lottie entered first and Thomas waited several minutes so that no one would suspect they had been walking together alone.

Lottie sat in a chair set apart from the table to watch the next round of cribbage, but deliberately far away from Mr. de Lacy.

Undeterred, Mr. de Lacy stood and sat beside her, flicking his fingers at Thomas. "Fetch me a drink."

Thomas bowed, his eyes flickering darkly, but he obeyed.

Lottie glowered at Mr. de Lacy and lifted her chin primly. It still set her on edge to see Edmund's face again... or at least, a face so similar.

In silence, they watched the game together, Thomas standing protectively at Lottie's shoulder. Slowly, Lottie realized that something about the game was bothering her.

"What is it?" Mr. de Lacy leaned closer.

Thomas growled low in his throat.

Lottie blinked, watching the game more closely. Sir Roland picked up another card, his ears reddening and his eyes narrowing as if pleased. Lord Campbell shifted, lifting one fist to cough discreetly. As he did so, he slipped a new card out of his sleeve and into his hand.

But neither of those moments were what had caught Lottie's eye. She sucked in a breath. Once again, Miss Wilde reached for a new card with her right hand. Then she picked up her pencil and wrote her bet on one of the slips of paper.

"She's not left-handed," Lottie whispered to herself.

***Hey friends! Since it seems that Octavia didn't kill Mr. Farraday, who do you think did it?

I'd love to hear your thoughts! If you enjoyed this chapter, don't forget to vote and comment!

A Scotsman's Heart

Thomas reached a hand out to Lottie's shoulder but stopped himself just in time.

Mr. de Lacy's gaze flicked between them and his lips twitched knowingly. Thomas's chest grew hot with annoyance at the insinuating grin.

Lottie rose to her feet, determination pinching her brows.

"Lottie," Thomas whispered. She glanced back at him and he shook his head slightly.

Mr. de Lacy stood as well and leaned close to Lottie. "Care to share your revelation?" His arm brushed her shoulder. Thomas strangled a growl, his eyes widening in outrage.

Lottie glared at Mr. de Lacy and pointedly stepped away, but Thomas still found himself breathing heavily. How dare Mr. de Lacy pretend such intimacy with his Lottie?

My Lottie... Thomas's shoulders sagged slightly as he realized that he had no right to call the beautiful young woman his. He was a lowly stable-boy-turned-valet, not someone with wealth or good social standing worthy of Miss Lottie Atwell, the sought-after charge of Lord Greyville.

Before Mr. de Lacy could try to interrogate Lottie again, Mrs. Ashdown excused herself from the card table and looped her arm through his, dragging him toward the side chairs.

"Oh, dear Mr. de Lacy, I have some juicy gossip that I think you will find most intriguing," her eyes glittered meaningfully in Lottie's direction, but Thomas found his attention drawn to the remaining players at the table.

Lord Campbell and Lady Hillington both watched the older woman with shadowed faces.

With the round ended, the Countess and Earl bid their guests goodnight and the players retired for the evening.

Lottie followed, her attention solely on Miss Wilde. Thomas groaned inwardly. Was she about to confront another suspected murderer? Had his warning only an hour before meant nothing to her?

Discretely, he followed after her as she stalked Miss Wilde through the dark castle halls. Their prey happily tucked her winnings into her bodice, looking more at ease than Thomas had seen her thus far.

Miss Wilde slipped into her room, and, with an annoyed grumble, Thomas watched as Lottie followed so closely behind that she entered before the door could close. Her footsteps must have been silent enough that Miss Wilde hadn't heard.

*** Lottie closed the door with a soft click behind her, watching Miss Wilde's every move.

"Is Mrs. Ashdown aware that you are not her beloved niece?" she asked quietly.

Miss Wilde screamed, whirling around so fast that some of her carefully pinned curls flew loose.

The door behind Lottie burst open, throwing her forward.

She landed hard on the wood floor, her elbow taking most of the fall. Thomas exploded into the room, the spiked ball of a Morning Star swinging from his raised hand as he yelled fearsomely.

Miss Wilde and Lottie screamed simultaneously. Thomas stumbled back in surprise at their shrill voices, the Morning Star wavering. He must have stolen it from one of the many suits of armor that lined the hallway, Lottie thought even as her heart pounded from the shock of seeing him rush through like some Scottish warrior from the Highlands.

Miss Wilde dropped to the floor in a dead faint and Thomas grimaced guiltily.

"Lottie?" he whispered, looking rather sheepish as he held the medieval weapon to his chest to keep the wickedly spiked ball from swinging.

"Down here," Lottie huffed, holding up her hand expectantly.

"Oh!" Thomas grinned awkwardly and pulled her to her feet. "How did ye end up down there?"

"How do you think?" Lottie raised her brows at him and thrust her hand toward the door.

"Oh," Thomas said again, his cheeks reddening. "In my defense, I did believe ye were in mortal danger."

Lottie sighed and patted him on the arm. "My brave, brave Scotsman, coming to my rescue from a faint-hearted woman half my size."

Thomas puffed his chest and winked. "I was very brave, wasn't I?"

Rolling her eyes, Lottie turned back to Miss Wilde, who was still laying on the floor in a dead faint. "Help me get her onto a chair?" she asked as she tugged at one of the woman's thin hands.

Thomas lifted the woman awkwardly and set her in a chair beside the dark fireplace while Lottie retrieved a cup of water from the vanity. They exchanged glances and Lottie shrugged, dipping her fingers into the water and flicked it on Miss Wilde's cheeks.

Slowly, Miss Wilde blinked and looked up at Lottie. "Oh, Miss Lottie," she sighed, still sagged in the chair. "I had the strangest dream. This big Scottish brute burst through my door swinging a spiked ball, and—" her gaze shifted to Thomas, who wiggled his fingers, looking for all the world like a little boy who had been caught sneaking cookies from the kitchen.

"Oh, bollocks," Miss Wilde squeaked.

Lottie pushed Thomas aside with her hip and stood over the other woman, crossing her arms in an attempt to appear imposing. "Now, Miss Wilde... if that even is your name, please answer my question. Does Mrs. Ashdown know that you are not her niece?"

The mousy woman's eyes widened. She shifted in her seat, sitting ramrod straight. "I... I don't know what you're talking about."

Lottie sighed and rolled her eyes. She grasped Miss Wilde's left wrist, holding it up so that they could see her hand. "Mrs. Ashdown showed me a letter written to her by her beloved niece, supposedly written just before the woman embarked on a ship in the Caribbean. The letters were smudged, the way the ink smears when the writer is left-handed. Surely, Mrs. Ashdown has received many letters over the years and would notice if the handwriting was different at all."

Miss Wilde paled, looking frantically between Lottie and Thomas, who still held the Morning Star over his shoulder. "I... I wrote them."

Lottie shook her head, tightening her hold on the thin wrist. "You wrote your bets at the card table with your right hand. See? No smudges on your left hand. Come to think of it... you always use your right hand, never the left."

Mouth opening and closing, Miss Wilde shook her head.

"Where is the real Miss Wilde?" Lottie released the woman's hand. "Who are you?"

Finally, the imposter burst into tears. She covered her face and pulled her legs up onto the chair in a way no proper young woman would have. "My name is Heather Lucas, I was sent with Miss Wilde to her Uncle's plantation in the Caribbean ten years ago after her parents died."

Lottie stepped back in surprise. She had not anticipated the woman being a mere maid in disguise. "Then... you...?"

"I didn't want to do it, but she forced me!" Heather clasped Lottie's hands desperately. "Please, you must believe me. Miss Wilde fell in love with a man who worked on the plantation. She knew her family would never approve, and when Mrs. Ashdown sent for her... she panicked. She wrote a letter to her aunt saying she would be on the next boat out, and then she put me on the ship in one of her dresses and escaped with that man. I don't know where she is now, but I—I was too afraid to reveal the truth."

Numbly, Lottie sat on the arm of the chair, her hands still held captive by the frantic young woman. "I suppose that makes sense," she said, nodding slowly. "Did Mr. Farraday know?"

Heather grew even paler. "How did you—?"

"That was what he whispered to you the first night of the house party, wasn't it? He knew that you were not the real Miss Wilde. But how?" Lottie asked.

Heather shook her head and dropped her gaze. "It had been ten years since anyone in England had seen Miss Wilde. We share similar hair and eye color, and everyone assumed that any other differences were simply the result of outgrowing childhood. But... one of the plantation supervisors returned to England not long after I did to visit his dying father. He saw me. I suppose Mr. Farraday found out somehow... he said he had all the evidence in that blasted notebook of his."

"What did he want?" Thomas asked, drawing closer to Lottie's side.

"Miss Wilde's dowery," Heather sniffled. "He wanted me to get it from Mrs. Ashdown. But... I think Mrs. Ashdown knows that I am not her niece. She acted so strangely the first day I returned, and one time she even called me 'Heather' by accident, and yet... yet she has still been so kind to me. I suspect she is just lonely. I did not want to betray her and I even tried to tell Mr. Farraday that on the morning that he left, but he ignored me—"

"The morning he left?" Lottie interrupted.

"Yes," Heather faltered as if confused by the other young woman's sharp tone. "I saw the back of him in his coat and hat as he was leaving... sometime after dawn, I believe."

Lottie's shoulders slumped. But how could that be? He was dead before then!

Thomas pulled her aside, eyeing Heather cautiously as he whispered, "Lord Campbell said the same thing."

Lottie chewed her thumbnail thoughtfully. "Miss Wilde—er, Heather, did you notice anything else about him? Did you see his face?"

Heather tipped her head thoughtfully. "I never saw his face... but he was all muddy and wet."

*** Thomas and Lottie apologized to Heather for startling her so badly and quickly big goodnight. As he walked beside her, warmth spread through his chest as his arm brushed her shoulder, and he was gratified that she didn't pull away as she had with Mr. de Lacy.

"Foolish girl," Lottie muttered, shaking her head.

"Heather?" Thomas asked, the Morning Star still hanging from his hand. He would need to return it to the suit of armor he had stolen it from in his haste to protect Lottie.

"Miss Wilde. The real Miss Wilde, I mean," Lottie said with a sigh. "How could she run off with a man who claimed to love her?"

Thomas paused, his gaze dropping. He sensed her words had more weight than she let on. After all, hadn't Edmund de Lacy claimed to love her in order to kidnap her?

Finally, they reached the suit of armor he had borrowed the weapon from and he returned it. As they stared at the ancient armor together, Thomas leaned his side against hers comfortingly. "Do ye nae believe in love now, wee lassie?"

Lottie sighed and rested her head on his shoulder. "When Fidelia and William were forced to marry, it seemed to me the most romantic thing, like in a story. I knew they would fall desperately in love. In my childish heart, I suppose I also wanted to feel that 'magical' thing called love. I doted upon Edmund as if he were a knight in shining armor... always there to rescue me."

Hearing Lottie speak about another man in such a way made Thomas shift uncomfortably, even though he knew that Edmund had betrayed her. For a time, the coward had been everything to Lottie, Thomas knew. "Ye loved him."

"I thought I loved him. Now I realize that I do not even know what the word means," Lottie stood straighter and suddenly pulled the breastplate from the suit of armor, leaving behind a barren gap in the stand. "Do you think this would provide good protection during my experiments?"

She hurried down the hallway in the direction of her laboratory. Thomas opened his mouth to call after her, but he was afraid to alert any of the servants to their presence. He followed her up the spiral stairs and out onto the castle roof. She clutched the breastplate to her chest, staring out at the ocean in the distance as she walked along the buttress.

"Wee lassie," Thomas caught her hand and gently pulled her to a stop. She refused to face him. A freezing wind blew over the wall and she shivered slightly. With a sigh, Thomas wrapped his arms around her, holding her tightly against the chill. "I ken ye are trying to hide from what happened with Edmund. I'm sorry for bringing up such painful memories."

Slowly, Lottie leaned back into his embrace, her head fitting perfectly beneath his chin. It felt so natural to hold her that Thomas could almost forget the impropriety of the touch.

"It is hard to believe I used to be such a romantic," she said quietly. "Now... I have resigned myself to being alone. After all, what man would want to marry a woman whose mind is always spinning with inventions? A woman whose reputation will be ruined if anyone finds out about Edmund and Le Coquin?"

I do, Thomas thought, and it made his heart constrict painfully. "Wee lassie," he began, tightening his arms around her and nestling his cheek against her soft hair. "If... if there were such a man... would ye accept his love for ye?"

Lottie was silent for a moment as if seriously considering it. "Love," she spat, pulling away from him and slapping a hand on the stone wall. "I hate that word. It is just a word men use to trick women. They think they can anything they want if they say 'I love you,' and we foolish women believe that they mean it."

The words stung. Thomas forced a rough "huh," of laughter to hide how his heart hurt at her dismissal, but his head bowed. Lottie had been so deeply wounded by Edmund... would she ever believe that Thomas earnestly cared for her? Or would his lowly position as a servant keep them apart anyway?

Feeling like the floor was dropping out from under him, Thomas realized that he may never be able to prove to her that she had slowly become everything to him. But that could not keep him from protecting her at a distance. He could still care for her and help her. He would never expect anything in return, he decided.

Gently, he slid the breastplate from her hand. "I can make this fit ye better. It will be more comfortable that way during yer experiments," he said in a soft voice.

Lottie looked over her shoulder at him, a small smile turning up one corner of her lips. "You are a good friend, Thomas."

I wish I had the right to be more, Thomas thought even as he returned her smile.

*** Lottie slept fitfully that night, her dreams haunted by misshapen memories of Edmund and Mr. Farraday. No matter how tightly she pulled the blankets around herself, she still felt cold. She had felt chilled since the moment she had pulled from Thomas's warm, comforting embrace that evening.

Sally's frantic voice pierced her dreams. Someone tugged her into a sitting position.

"Lottie, wake up!" Octavia said, her voice strong and quiet with urgency.

Groggily, Lottie blinked to find Sally and Octavia in her bedroom. It was still dark. She must not have slept longer than an hour or so. "What's wrong?" she mumbled, rubbing sleep from her eyes.

"It's Mrs. Ashdown..." Octavia said, swallowing hard. "She's been murdered."

***Hey guys! Thank you for being patient with this late update! But don't worry, I am back to the regular MWF schedule now :D

What did you think of Miss Wilde's secret? And do you think Lottie will realize that Thomas is in love with her? Can she love him back? I'd love to hear your thoughts!

Poison and Secret Identities

Lottie stared at Octavia in horror. "Another murder? B-but how? When?"

The other two women pulled Lottie to her feet and Sally helped her dress while Octavia explained.

"Miss Wilde just found Mrs. Ashdown in the ballroom. Mr. de Lacy has demanded your presence for questioning."

Lottie paused, her loose hair pulled halfway over her shoulder. "Me? Why?"

"He wouldn't say. No one else is allowed into the ballroom. Only you," Octavia said. She was eerily calm about the situation, but her face was pale and drawn. "Do you think..." she paused, swallowing hard again. "Do you think that the blackmailer is killing those of us who cannot give them what they want?"

Shaking her head, Lottie lead the way to the ballroom in silence. Was Octavia right? Had the killer struck again because Mrs. Ashdown hadn't given in to his demands? But Miss Wilde—Heather was the one who was being blackmailed. Why kill Mrs. Ashdown?

Two men that Lottie didn't recognize guarded the door to the ballroom, keeping William, the Countess, and the Earl at bay.

"I am the Earl of Durham," the Earl blustered, doing his best to seem imposing. "How dare you block me in my own house!"

But the men's faces remained stoic.

"My men are under strict orders, Your Grace," Mr. de Lacy said as he stepped into the doorway, wiping his hands on a handkerchief. "This is a murder investigation, after all."

William spotted Lottie and tried to wave her back, but Mr. de Lacy spotted the movement and followed the lord's gaze. "Ah," his eyes narrowed. "Miss Lottie. Please, do come in."

William held his hand out to stop her as she pushed forward. "How dare you, Mr. de Lacy?" he said, his voice low and dangerous. "Lottie is a young lady and my charge. How can you ask her to view such a horrific scene alone?"

"If my suspicions are correct," Mr. de Lacy's voice purred, "then she has already seen it. Come along, Miss Lottie."

Lottie looked around at the concerned faces of the people who loved her dearly. Clutching her hands together, she nodded at her brother-in-law and forced a smile. "It's alright, William."

He growled, balling his hands into fists. "I must find Thomas," he muttered, storming off.

Leaving the rest of them behind, Lottie followed Mr. de Lacy into the dark ballroom. Pale, wintry moonlight pooled in from the tall windows on her left, illuminating ghostly patches on the marble floor... and Mrs. Ashdown.

She lay in the middle shaft of light, on her back, staring blankly up at the ceiling. Lottie gasped and turned aside, closing her eyes tightly against the sight. This was her second time seeing a dead body within a week, but it was far more shocking than finding Mr. Farraday.

"Take a good look, Miss Lottie," Mr. de Lacy ordered, turning her back toward the body. "Tell me, what does your scientific mind see?"

Trembling, Lottie forced her eyes open and peered at the unfortunate woman. Had Lottie not already known she was dead, it would have appeared the woman was simply resting... with her eyes open. Nothing looked out of the ordinary... except...

"Her skin... is it blue? Or is that a trick of the moonlight?" Lottie asked, her voice a whisper.

He nodded, kneeling beside the body and pointing to her lips. "Here, too. And there was foam, but someone wiped it off as if to hide the true cause of her death."

Lottie dropped her gaze. "What killed her, then?"

"Poison. Deadly nightshade, if I were a betting man," Mr. de Lacy lifted the woman's hand, which was clenched into a fist.

"What's that in her hand?" Lottie asked, crouching beside him.

He smiled as if pleased that her keen eye had caught the tiny clue. "A scrap of parchment. I refrained from looking at it until you arrived."

"Why?" Lottie asked, the hairs on the back of her neck prickling.

"To see your reaction." He pried Mrs. Ashdown's fingers open and removed a crumpled, yellowed piece of parchment. Slowly, he smoothed it out on the floor, and they examined it together. It appeared to be the front half of two lines, the rest of the message ripped away.

"The lord knows... she can't hide anymore..." Lottie read aloud, unease pooling in her gut.

Mr. de Lacy hummed to himself, tapping the 'she' on the paper. "Care to explain what you cannot hide anymore, Miss Lottie?"

She shook her head slowly. "I've hardly spoken more than a few sentences to Mrs. Ashdown in her whole time here. How could she...? I have nothing to hide, Mr. de Lacy," she said, the lie forming a lump in her throat. The truth about Edmund's death, finding Mr. Farraday's body, knowing the location of the first murder... they were all things she had to hide, but it was impossible for Mrs. Ashdown to know about anything of them.

He narrowed his eyes. "That's not what she led me to believe earlier this evening when she pulled me aside to gossip. Wouldn't you like to know what she said about you?"

Lottie pushed to her feet. "I have done nothing to Mrs. Ashdown, Mr. de Lacy. She was a gossip, it is true, but she was just a lonely old woman looking for entertainment and company. I had no grudges against her." Her voice was firm even as her hands shook.

"De Lacy!" Thomas's voice thundered from the doorway.

*** The short men from the magistrate's office that guarded the entry to the ballroom were no match for Thomas's broad shoulders and tall frame. He easily shoved them aside and stormed into the dark ballroom.

Lottie spun around, her long, loose hair flashing silver in the moonlight. Her shoulders sagged in relief at the sight of him and she ran to meet him.

Thomas wrapped an arm around her shoulder for only a moment before turning her behind him. "Stay here," he whispered, his eyes never leaving Mr. de Lacy.

He grabbed the man by his cravat, shoving him back a step. "What games are ye playing at?" he growled.

Mr. de Lacy smirked, leaning in closer. "No games, Mr. Hawthorne, just searching for the truth."

"Lottie has nothing to do with this," Thomas tightened his hand, forcing himself not to look at the dead body.

"On the contrary," Mr. de Lacy held up a torn scrap of paper. "It seems she has everything to do with this."

Thomas read the words and his chest tightened. "There are plenty of women at this house party. Mrs. Ashdown could have been referring to any of them."

Mr. de Lacy finally shoved Thomas's hand away. He straightened his cravat and smoothed his hair. "The other half of the note provides just as much insight."

Thomas blinked, unsure of what the man was implying. "I'm warning ye, de Lacy... leave Lottie alone." He grabbed Lottie's hand and pulled her toward the door. She looked stunned as if the sight of the body had thrown her into shock. Thomas had seen more than his fair share of the dead during his time at war... but it never got easier.

"You seem to forget something rather important," Mr. de Lacy said coolly behind them. "I was acquainted with all of Edmund's friends... Mr. Hawthorne."

Thomas froze, the ground swaying behind him. 'the lord knows...' the words churned in his mind. Did Mr. de Lacy think that referred to Thomas's identity?

Without looking back, Thomas wrapped an arm around Lottie and escorted her out of the ballroom. The hallway was empty now as if the guards had ushered William's family away.

"How did you know I was here?" Lottie asked, her voice small.

"William told me. With Fidelia's condition, there is very little he can risk in challenging the local magistrate. I, on the other hand, am but a lowly servant, and have nothing to lose," he winked at the young woman under his arm.

She didn't smile at his light tone. "What did he mean when he said he knew all of Edmund's friends?"

Thomas slowed, his eyes growing out of focus slightly. He had pushed the memories of his past so far aside that he had almost convinced himself he had always been Thomas Hawthorne, the lowly stable hand.

"Did you..." Lottie shifted from under his arm, turning to face him. "Did you know Edmund?"

Thomas stared above her head down the hallway. "Aye," he said quietly. "Aye, I knew him. But that was many years ago."

Lottie clenched her hands together. "Why didn't you tell me? How did you—"

"Mr. de Lacy seems convinced you were responsible for Mrs. Ashdown's death," Thomas interrupted, taking her hands in his. "We have more important things to consider. I swear to explain everything later. First... what was the meaning of that note?"

Her brows pinched together, but she seemed to agree to the sharp change in subject. "It mentioned both the Lord in Heaven and a mysterious 'she...' but I do not know who Mrs. Ashdown meant. Mr. de Lacy said that she had spoken to him about me—"

"Not the Lord in Heaven," Thomas said suddenly, snapping his fingers. "The 'L' was not capitalized. Perhaps she meant a titled lord?"

"There are only Lord Greyville and Lord Campbell here in the castle," Lottie said, nodding slowly.

There is another, Thomas thought silently, but Mrs. Ashdown couldn't have possibly known. Aloud, he said, "when she pulled Mr. de Lacy aside to speak, I noticed both Lady Hillington and Lord Campbell seemed to be particularly concerned. A lord and a woman."

"We should start there," Lottie agreed.

*** Mrs. Ashdown's death threw the guests into a buzz the next morning at breakfast. Lottie had expected them to become frightened and leave the house party, but instead, the tragedy seemed like a novelty to them all. To everyone except for Heather Lucas and Octavia, that is. The rest of the guests twittered about it excitedly, and Sir Roland recounted every interaction he had had with the dead woman with particularly great relish.

"Are you alright?" Lottie whispered to Heather, taking the small woman's hand as they sat at the far end of the table, away from the rest.

Heather shook her head, tears brimming in her eyes. "How could she just die?" Heather cried, burying her head in her hands. "She was just fine last night!"

Lottie tipped her head, confused. "Just...die?" she glanced toward Mr. de Lacy, who caught her gaze and shook his head slightly. Had he not told any of the guests that it was a murder? Octavia and the rest of Lottie's family that had gathered at the ballroom door had known Mrs. Ashdown had been killed... could the truth be contained from the rest for long?

"Did she act... strangely?" Lottie asked, trying not to give away what she knew. Heather seemed distraught enough as it was, she would probably faint if she learned that her pretend aunt had been murdered.

Heather thought for a moment, dabbing at her nose with a handkerchief. "She seemed so excited a few days ago. She kept saying I wouldn't need to marry and that she had a way of getting enough money for us to live comfortably all our lives."

"How?" Lottie asked eagerly.

The mousy woman shrugged. "She said she saw something the night before Mr. Farraday left... but she wouldn't tell me anything more than that."

Patting the mournful woman's hand comfortingly, Lottie let her gaze slide toward Lady Hillington. She seemed pale, even as she pretended to join in the sadistic discussion of Mrs. Ashdown's untimely death. She hadn't seemed particularly close with the dead woman... but her pallor didn't appear to be from sorrow. Rather, she seemed fretful, twisting her wedding ring on her finger and glancing fervently at her son.

Lottie would have to take a gamble, she decided.

After breakfast, the group decided to take a stroll through the hedge maze since the morning was unseasonably warm. Lottie trailed along slightly behind the rest, waiting until Lady Hillington stopped to examine a statue of a praying angel.

Lottie drew close, pretending to admire the statue as well. Leaning in, she whispered. "Mrs. Ashdown knew your secret, didn't she? That's why you killed her."

***Hey guys!

DUN DUN DUN! Another murder!

What did you think of Mr. de Lacy and Thomas in this chapter? I'd love to hear your thoughts! Thank you for reading this far, I absolutely love reading your comments!

Affairs and Threats

Lady Hillington froze, staring at the statue. Slowly, she turned to face Lottie, and she smirked. "Do not think you can intimidate me like the others, little girl."

Lottie's confident smile vanished. Oh, dear, she thought, backing up a step. "O-others?"

"Did you think your little investigation was so secretive?" Lady Hillington laughed demurely, folding her hands together at her waist. She lifted her chin. "I've seen you watching us all, following us, prying into our secrets just like that scrawny weasel, Farraday. I know it was you who snuck into my room and rifled through my wardrobe. The bloody sand was a dead giveaway."

Hands balling into fists, Lottie swallowed. Bloody sand? That was the same as Octavia's room. Whoever it was, they had searched both rooms. Had they searched Lottie's as well? Since she couldn't frighten Lady Hillington into revealing her secrets, perhaps it was best to play along. "Yes," Lottie lied. "It was me."

"So, you managed to kill him? I don't believe it for a moment," Lady Hillington scoffed. "But you are the one who was trying to dig up my secrets to blackmail me."

"Farraday?" Lottie backed up another step. "You know he's dead?"

Lady Hillington narrowed her eyes. "Of course I do. Those little letters you've been sending me, trying to blackmail me just like he did, were obviously in different handwriting. A man like him would never give up so easily. Death was the only explanation."

The letters. Lottie had received one from the new blackmailer, and so had Octavia. Now, it seemed Lady Hillington was also one of the killer's new targets. "If you don't believe I could have killed him, why do you think I'm the blackmailer?"

"Mrs. Ashdown wasn't the only one who saw you with blood on your hands the morning he disappeared. But you found him after the fact, didn't you?"

The woman's sharp observations made the hairs on Lottie's neck stand up under her thick winter cloak. But what blood was she referring to? Thomas had cleaned the blood from Lottie's hands before she returned to the castle...

"Tell me," Lady Hillington advanced, her hair deathly grey in the wintry sunlight. Shadows cast by her brows made her eyes look pouchy and dark. "How did you find out about my son?"

Lottie's gaze darted around. Thomas's warning from the other night suddenly sounded much more logical. Lady Hillington looked frightfully dangerous. "Y-your son?" Of course, the woman doted so lovingly upon Captain Hillington, it seemed logical that harm to him could be the only thing that would frighten her.

"My husband would never believe you," Lady Hillington's voice wavered in spite of her fierce words.

Looking over her shoulder at the empty passageways of the maze, Lottie's mind raced. She had to gain the upper hand here before she wound up like Mrs. Ashdown. "He's... illegitimate, isn't he?" It was a wild guess, but it was the only thing that she could think of given the embarrassed flush of the woman's face.

Lady Hillington gawked. Her frightening expression vanished, and her shoulders sank. "You really did know. Mrs. Ashdown told you, didn't she?"

Slowly, Lottie nodded. It was a lie, of course, but perhaps she could get the truth from Lady Hillington at last. "She was going to tell the father first, but you know how she gossips..." She shrugged, hoping that would imply whatever Lady Hillington was fearing the most.

"It will do you no good to tell Sir Roland. He's an even bigger moron now than he was back then," Lady Hillington snorted, turning back to the statue even as she clutched her hands tighter together.

Lottie slapped a hand over her mouth to silence a gasp, horror, disgust, and fascination warring within her. Lady Hillington had had an affair with Sir Roland of all people? That short, nose-picking man with a gut made large by far too many alcoholic drinks? "Yes... Sir Roland," Lottie agreed lamely. "Mrs. Ashdown knew because—"

"How could she have claimed to be my friend?" Lady Hillington's voice quavered. "She was there, all those years ago when I met him. I was so lonely, you see, and it was just a game, until—but she swore to protect my secret. I never dreamed she would betray me."

Lottie's mind churned. So, Mrs. Ashdown really had known about Lady Hillington's dark secret since she had witnessed the beginning of the affair, but could that have been where Mr. Farraday learned of it? Or did he have another source? "Is that why you killed her? Because she betrayed you?"

Turning, the now-haggard woman stared at Lottie with teary eyes. "I didn't kill her. I just... I wiped the foam from her lips after I found her in the ballroom last night. She said she was going to meet someone who would ensure her future. I followed along because I was afraid she was going to tell my secrets. By the time I arrived... she was already gone. I know I should not have touched her after she'd been killed... But I just wanted my friend to be at peace."

"Who was she meeting with?" Lottie asked gently, touching the woman's shoulder in a comforting gesture. She seemed so broken and distraught now.

Lady Hillington shook her head mournfully. "I don't know. I just saw the back of them when they left. It looked... like Mr. Farraday. It was his hat and cloak, but surely he must be dead, so it is entirely illogical."

Lottie caught her breath. This was the third time someone mentioned seeing Mr. Farraday after his death. Someone must be pretending to be him... unless Mr. Farraday had never died at all. Lottie immediately dismissed that thought. She had seen the blood in the laboratory and the large cut on his chest at the beach. There was no way he could have survived.

"I'm not the blackmailer, Lady Hillington. And I swear to never reveal your secret," Lottie said quietly.

***

In the drawing-room later that evening, Lottie mulled over Lady Hillington's revelations as she sat with the guests. She had found bloodied sand in her own room, buried amongst the things in the chest by her bed. Whoever had searched the rooms must have left it by accident in their haste. They must have done it just after they moved the body to the new location.

She had also found the tip of a muddy splotch that smelled slightly of manure on the floor underneath the chest as if the unknown intruder had moved it, knelt, and left behind a trace while looking under her bed.

"What has you so pensive?" Fidelia asked as she sank onto the settee beside Lottie. Since some color had returned to her cheeks and she had been able to keep down her meals that day, the doctor had allowed her to leave her wheeled chair after dinner and walk about the room for a bit. It must have tired her, however, for sweat plastered a few coppery curls to her forehead.

Lottie smiled and clasped her sister's hand. "Nothing. Just... missing Charles," the lie came so easily to her lips that she wondered if it was because she had been lying so often these days. But she couldn't let Fidelia worry about anything more than her health and growing her precious child. Such a task seemed difficult enough already, judging by her weakened constitution.

Fidelia brightened. "William told me this morning that he has sent inquiries to all of his contacts remaining in America to look for Charles if they can. I'm sure we will have news in a few months."

Hope surged in her chest. "Truly?"

Fidelia nodded, casting an adoring gaze at her husband, who stood talking with Lord Campbell and the Earl across the room.

"I couldn't help but overhear news about the mysterious Charles Atwell," Octavia joined them, sitting in the chair across from them, her eyes sparkling merrily. "Do tell."

Lottie repeated Fidelia's news and Octavia sat straighter. "You never speak of him much. It must be something truly promising if you are both so hopeful."

Fidelia sighed, leaning her head on Lottie's shoulder as if growing more tired. "It was excruciating to leave America without him. We were thick as thieves, the three of us. But he did what he did to protect us."

"What did he do?" Octavia leaned forward, eager for a taste of gossip.

Lottie exchanged a glance with Fidelia. They could never reveal that Charles, serving in the American military, had captured William at the start of the war. Once he realized it was his childhood friend, he had released the lord, begging him to rescue his sisters who were about to be trapped in a riot in Baltimore.

If the sisters ever spoke about it, it could reveal William's identity as a spy... and endanger Charles if the news ever reached America that he had intentionally let a prisoner of war go free.

"Did I ever tell you about the time he tried to braid my hair after mother died?" Lottie changed the subject abruptly, hoping to divert Octavia's nosy interest.

Octavia laughed, covering her mouth delicately. "A man doing a little girl's hair? I've never heard of such a thing."

Fidelia smiled sadly, her eyes growing unfocused. "He was the gentlest man I'd ever met. Other than William, of course. He took it upon himself to care for us as a mother, teaching us how to do our hair... helping us with the chores at the eatery, acting as our confidante, always listening to our secrets..." her voice faded away.

Lottie looked at their clasped hands. It had been so painful to think about where Charles could be. In over a year, the only news they had of him was that he had been dishonorably discharged. She had forced herself to not think of him so many times that it had become second nature.

Octavia sighed wistfully. "Ah, do not tempt me, my dears. If I knew such a man existed, I might be tempted away from my prize," her gaze rested on Captain Hillington meaningfully as he sat with Mr. de Lacy near the pianoforte.

*** As Lottie brushed her hair before her mirror, preparing for bed, memories of Charles made her hands slow. Tears blurred her vision and she set the brush down, remembering the way he had brushed her hair with slow, awkward movements the day after their mother's death. He had been the one to teach her how to drive a wagon. He had been the one to protect her after their father's death.

Until rumors of war wove through Baltimore, and he was coerced to enlist by the local regiment. If only he had stayed. Perhaps none of this would have happened. We need you here, Charles. I need you here. You would know what to do.

Frantic knocking roused her from her thoughts, and she brushed away her tears.

Opening the door, she found Octavia with a letter clasped in her hands. "I'm next. He says I am next. I'm doomed, Lottie!"

Lottie pulled her inside quickly, looking around the hallway carefully before closing the door.

"Tell me everything," she ordered as she sat her friend before the dying fireplace.

With shaking hands, Octavia held out the crumpled note. "The blackmailer said to give him what he wants, or I'll be the next one found poisoned."

Lottie read the note several times over, her heart stuttering. Finally, she threw it to the ground. "I will not let him kill you. I am getting you out of here. Tonight."

***Hey guys! Lady Hillington and Sir Roland, eh? What a strange surprise!

And I hope you enjoyed getting a glimpse of Charles! This is leading into the next book, which centers on Charles, Octavia, and pirates. (Psst, he's much more of a devilish rogue than Fidelia and Lottie let Octavia believe ;)

If you liked this chapter, please be sure to vote and comment! You rock!

Disguised As A Man

Thomas paused to wipe his brow as he bent over the anvil. Since Fidelia was feeling better that day, William had given Thomas the time off to work on reshaping the breastplate from the suit of armor for Lottie.

The door to the smithy creaked and he tightened his grip on the hammer. The blackmailer. Slowly, he placed the breastplate down and crept closer to the entrance.

He shoved the door open with his shoulder, raising the hammer to strike.

Two high-pitched squeals stopped him just in time as Lottie and Octavia fell to the ground, covering their heads.

"Wee lassie," he huffed and his shoulders sagged. "Have ye no sense of self-preservation? Sneaking up on someone working in the forge," he muttered and pulled them to their feet. "Going to get yerselves killed."

"We looked everywhere for you," Lottie explained as she ushered them inside the small smithy. It was designed for smaller projects, such as sharpening swords or shoeing the horses, and the tools worked well enough for reshaping the piece of armor. "We weren't sure if it would really be you in here, so we hesitated..."

"What's the matter?" Thomas asked as he put away his tools. "Ye lassies look like wee ghosts in the night."

"The blackmailer sent another note," Octavia said quietly. "I'll be the next to die if he doesn't get what he wants."

Thomas drew a deep breath. "Nae on my watch."

"I knew you'd help us," Lottie cried in relief, throwing her hands around his neck.

He lost all power over words, surprised at her sudden affection. Ears burning pleasantly, he grinned. "Come now, lassie. T'is nae the time. What be yer bold plan?"

Awkwardly, Lottie released him and glanced back at Octavia, who stood with her arms around herself, pale and stunned.

"I... don't have a plan. I just know we need to get her out of here before she ends up like Mr. Farraday or Mrs. Ashdown," Lottie said taking Octavia's hand.

"I cannot leave," Octavia whispered, shaking her head. "What about my father? The blackmailer will just go after my parents if I disappear."

Lottie chewed her thumbnail and paced. "The blackmailer is getting desperate. His murder of Mrs. Ashdown proves that. With the magistrate here investigating, he must feel as if he is becoming cornered. I am certain that I can expose him before the end of this house party... assuming no one else dies."

Thomas watched her, his heart sinking. She truly wasn't giving up on her fool-hearty search.

"He won't have a chance to go after your parents, I promise," Lottie said, pulling her shoulders back as if to prove her confidence.

Octavia sighed and sat on the only chair. "Even if the blackmailer is caught, my father still owes a substantial debt to his investors. I have been paying them out of my dowery, but I only have... nine months' worth. Perhaps ten if I can move my parents to a smaller cottage. Once the money runs out they will discover the truth about their investments and my father will be thrown into debtor's prison."

Thomas rubbed the stubble on his chin. "Have ye no other means of obtaining any money?"

She laughed sardonically and leaned back in the chair. "That trade agreement would be worth a pretty penny, but it was left behind on my father's ship when we were forced to abandon it in Baltimore."

"Is there any hope in retrieving it?" Lottie asked, kneeling beside her friend. It broke Thomas's heart to see how worried she was. If only Mr. Farraday's death had solved everything instead of making it worse.

Octavia's face clouded and she thought for a long moment. Slowly, she nodded. "If I could get to America, I could search for the ship. It was confiscated by the navy and would have been put into service for the war. The trade agreement was hidden in a secret, water-tight compartment in my father's quarters. No one would ever find it by accident."

"But how can ye, a lone woman, travel all the way to America and search for a ship in the service of an enemy navy?" Thomas asked.

Lottie's face fell.

"I can't," Octavia said quietly, "not as a woman." She stood and planted her fists on her hips. "But I could as a man."

Lottie snapped her fingers and jumped to her feet. "Dress as a man? Could that work?"

Thomas examined Octavia closely. "Ye be taller than most women, and have stronger features... I suppose ye could pass for a lad of fourteen or fifteen, but never as a grown man."

"I lived on my father's ships for most of my life. I can swagger and swear like any sailor," Octavia defended, lifting her chin.

Lottie grinned and patted her friend's hand kindly. "Yes, dearest, but you also have... other features that they do not. Pretending to be a boy rather than a man would make you less noticeable. The less they look at you, the better."

"Come along," Thomas gestured, leading the way out through the smithy, which was a separate building hidden behind the stables. The bright moon lit their way as wispy clouds drifted across its face. As they passed the backside of the stables, Lottie paused, staring at the manure piles.

"Don't you usually pile the manure all together? Why are there two separate piles?" She asked, cocking her head.

Thomas only spared a glance at the oddity, hurrying them along. "The new stable hand that William hired must be lazy," he said with a wink.

Once inside the stable, Thomas led them to the tack room. "I think I left some of my work clothes here when William moved the rest of my things to his valet's room. They were..." he paused and coughed with embarrassment. "I feared they were too smelly to bring into the castle."

He found the clothes just as he had left them, folded on the floor beneath the row of saddles. He slapped pointlessly at the dust and grime, then sheepishly held them out to Octavia.

She took them, turning her nose up slightly. "Um... thank you."

Lottie rolled her eyes at Thomas, but he just held up his hands defensively. "Do ye ken any other man's clothes ye can steal in the middle of the night?"

Octavia changed in one of the stables and returned several minutes later, her cheeks bright red. She had removed the pins from her hair, and it tumbled down her back in thick brown curls.

Lottie's hopeful expression faltered, and she glanced between Octavia and Thomas. "It's... not as convincing as I had hoped."

The trousers were far too long and puddled on the floor at her feet, and the shirt was so loose that she appeared to be drowning in it.

Frowning, Thomas nodded. "The trousers can be rolled to the right length, and a coat will cover the shirt... but I fear the hair is too obvious."

"I'll cut it then," Octavia said, pulling it over her shoulder. "Lottie, may I borrow your knife?"

Lottie frowned and sat her friend down on the floor. "It's such a shame. It's so lovely," she said as she fiddled with the hair as if unsure where to cut it.

"Cut it to the shoulder. She can tie it back, like Lord Greyville. It is a common style for boys on ships," Thomas instructed, gesturing for the length.

Lottie hesitated again and Octavia sighed, took the knife, and sawed at her hair. Strands fell to the floor as she made with work of her dark curls. The finished work hung slightly askew, but it was hardly noticeable when she tied it back at the nape of her neck with a piece of twine.

"Well?" she said, her cheeks no longer pink. She seemed more determined now, as if accepting there would be no going back from this.

"Dirty your cheeks," Thomas instructed, tapping his chin.

"What about Captain Hillington?" Lottie asked quietly as she helped Octavia smear dirt and grime on her cheeks to hide her feminine features. Now, she looked like a fine-boned, dirty boy in oversized clothes. At least the smell would keep most people farther away from her.

Octavia paused, her gaze falling to the floor. "Tell him I received news of my father's poor health. Tell him the engagement is off."

Lottie gasped, covering her mouth. "He proposed?"

Octavia nodded and tears of frustration brimmed in her eyes. "This morning. But his mother said she would never allow her son, a future lord, to marry the daughter of a merchant. She would cut him off entirely if he did. He even said we could elope and perhaps she would come around and give him his inheritance once the deed was done. Doubting that I could find another man with enough money to woo in time... I agreed. It was a gamble."

"Oh, Octavia," Lottie looped her arm through her friends and leaned her head on Octavia's shoulder. "I thought... I thought he really liked you."

"He does," Octavia swallowed hard and dashed the tears from her cheeks angrily. "But he doesn't deserve to be left in a lurch, wondering if or when I'll ever come back. And if anyone ever knew what I am about to do... my reputation would be destroyed beyond repair. He could never marry me now."

Thomas stepped away to give them privacy. Poor Captain Hillington would be heartbroken when he received the news. Thomas had noticed the way the man looked at Octavia. He saddled a couple of horses while the women said their tearful goodbyes, waiting with thick wool traveling cloaks.

"I'll ride with ye to the next town over," Thomas said, helping Octavia into the saddle. "Then I'll bring the horses back. It would be suspicious if one of the horses disappeared and it would be easier for the blackmailer to follow if he tries."

"Thank you," Octavia said, clasping Lottie's hand one last time. "Can you... can you check on my parents, Lottie? Tell them I'm alright and that I will fix everything."

"I promise," Lottie said. She pulled her cherry-handled knife from her pocket, as well as a small silver locket. "This knife belonged to Charles. If you find him, show him this and say you are a friend of mine. I'm sure he will help you as best he can. This locket contains a portrait of him from before he left for the war. It may help you find him."

Octavia nodded gratefully, donned the necklace, and tucked the knife into her waistband. "I'll tell him you're looking for him."

Thomas guided her to the side and Octavia turned away, pretending to fiddle with the saddle, but he appreciated her attempting to give them a moment.

"Go straight to yer room and lock the door," Thomas ordered, his voice quiet as he took Lottie's hand in both of his. "I will see ye when I return."

She nodded, her face somber. "Please take care of her. And... and come back safely. I... will miss you."

The corner of his lip lifted. "Are ye worried about me, lassie?"

She dropped her gaze and her cheeks tinged. "You are far too good to me, Thomas. How could I not worry for you?"

He cupped her cheek, brushing his thumb softly across her skin. Slowly, he leaned down and pressed a gentle kiss to her forehead.

***Gahhh sweet little kisses! We are nearing the end of our story, do you think they can make their romance work??

What do you think of Octavia's plan? I'd love to hear your thoughts!

Notebooks, Lies, and Catriona

L ottie pulled the blankets closer to her chin, staring up at the ceiling. The memory of Thomas's gentle kiss to her forehead replayed over in her mind and she curled her toes. Why did such a simple gesture of concern make her feel so giddy? Surely, Thomas meant nothing by it.

She rolled onto her side and covered her eyes. With a small squeal, she kicked her feet beneath the covers at the memory of his hand on her cheek.

"Oh, don't be a silly young girl," she ordered herself, pulling the covers over her head. "He meant nothing by it. He is simply a good friend showing his concern... by kissing me."

She rolled onto her other side and clamped her eyes closed tightly. No matter the butterflies in her stomach, her heart still refused to believe Thomas could have meant something more. She would ask him about it in the morning, she decided. If he made it back safely.

*** Lottie patted her hair again and smoothed her dress as she passed the library on her way to breakfast. Would Thomas be back by now? He had promised to check on her, but even though she woke to check her door several times throughout the night, there had been no sign of him.

"What are you implying, Mr. de Lacy?" Lord Campbell's angry voice echoed behind the closed door of the library and Lottie slowed.

"Several of the guests remember you leaving the drawing-room with Mr. Farraday the night he disappeared," Mr. de Lacy responded as Lottie pressed her ear to the door. "I am simply inquiring about your relationship with the man."

Silence. Could the men be speaking too quietly for her to hear through the door? She held her breath. Although she had cleared Lady Hillington of any involvement in Mrs. Ashdown's death, she hadn't had a moment to investigate Lord Campbell.

"He knew things he shouldn't," Lord Campbell's voice surprised Lottie and she pressed a hand over her mouth and nose to silence any sound that could alert the men. He continued, "Mr. Farraday had a proposition... a payment, if you will, for his silence on this... delicate matter."

Mr. de Lacy stepped closer to the door as he spoke, and Lottie wondered if he was going to open it. But instead, he said, "Mrs. Ashdown knew of this too, didn't she?"

"How did you--?" Lord Campbell's voice rose with shock.

"She told me. The night before her death," Mr. de Lacy responded casually. "She seemed quite eager to share the juicy details about everyone at the house party. She said she had more to share, but she died before she could."

Lord Campbell sighed and Lottie could hear his feet pacing. "You already know then."

"Naturally."

"And you suspect I had something to do with their murders?" Lord Campbell's voice was low and serious now.

"I have said nothing about murder, m'Lord," Mr. de Lacy said, but Lottie could hear a faint satisfaction in his tone.

"I-I they—They were—"

"Tell me what happened the nights they died. What did you do?" Mr. de Lacy asked.

After a long moment, Lord Campbell's voice finally broke. "I have substantial debts and have... caused the ruin of many young ladies. My father, the Duke of Argyle, threatened to cut me off unless I fixed my ways. I tricked my father for a time that I had repaid my debts and settled with the families of the women, but Mr. Farraday found out the truth somehow. The night before he died, he threatened to tell my father. He asked for my sister, but I refused. I countered."

"With what?" Mr. de Lacy scoffed, "he knew you were broke."

"My younger brother's inheritance," Lord Campbell said hesitantly. "He never returned from the war on the continent. My father would never know it was missing."

"And Mr. Farraday agreed to this?"

"Yes. We were going to visit my father's solicitor that morning, but I saw him just as he was leaving. He was in such a rush that he didn't even notice me when I called out to him."

Lottie tipped her head. That was almost word for word what Miss Wilde—er, Heather, had said. But she had never mentioned anything about seeing Lord Campbell there when Mr. Farraday left. Could one of them be lying?

"How did you know he died?" Mr. De Lacy asked.

"I went for a walk down to the beach later that morning," Lord Campbell's voice shuddered as if the memory sent shivers down his back. "I found a large pool of blood on the beach and marks as if the body had been dragged into the ocean. There were boot prints from a woman's shoe all around."

Dread pooled in Lottie's gut. Those were her boot prints, from when she had tripped over the body while walking in a stupor along the sand.

"And Mrs. Ashdown?" Mr. de Lacy prompted, as if unsurprised about the boot prints.

"She claimed to have information about my dalliances with the young ladies in a notebook. She wanted the payout I was going to give to Mr. Farraday in exchange for the evidence." Lord Campbell said. "I was going to meet her that night, but when I arrived at the ballroom, your men were already at the door. I surmised she must have been killed as well."

The notebook. Hadn't Mr. Farraday said his evidence against Lottie was in his notebook? But there had been nothing of the sort in Mrs. Ashdown's possession when Mr. de Lacy forced Lottie to examine the body with him. Could the torn scrap of paper clutched in her hand have come from the notebook? But if so... where was it now?

"May I leave now?" Lord Campbell asked anxiously.

Lottie quickly stepped away from the door. It would look terribly suspicious if she were caught by Mr. de Lacy eavesdropping on his interrogation.

She ran to the breakfast room, slowing only when she was within sight of the door. Her mind churned as she straightened her dress and smoothed her now-disgruntled hair. She was out of suspects. If everyone had an explanation for their involvement with Mr. Farraday and an excuse for their whereabouts around the time of his murder... then who was the real killer? Who was trying to blackmail her?

The rest of the guests were chatting amicably around the table as Lottie took her seat beside Catriona. The younger woman was silent and pensive, staring into her plate.

"Are you alright?" Lottie asked as a servant placed her food on the table.

"Where is Thomas?" Catriona asked quietly.

Lottie froze, her hand halfway toward her fork. "W-what do you mean?" she asked after a moment.

"Where did you send him?" Catriona snapped.

"Nowhere," Lottie replied, taken aback at the younger woman's sharp, frantic tone. Was she somehow close to Thomas?

"People around you keep dying," Catriona's voice dropped to a whisper and she leaned closer, her brown eyes, normally so doe-like, glowed dangerously. "If anything happens to him, I swear I will—"

Just then, Lord Campbell entered the room behind them and strode purposefully toward his sister. Captain Hillington, who sat on Catriona's other side, pushed his chair back to stand. The two men collided, bumping into the back of the young woman's chair.

Something flashed across the table and Lottie's eyes jumped to follow it, but it was too late. As she shifted her gaze back to the commotion behind Catriona, she vaguely noticed that the dark liquid in the young woman's teacup was swirling.

"Pardon me, old chap," Lord Campbell said, slapping Captain Hillington roughly on the shoulder.

The captain blinked at him in a daze, nodding slowly as his gaze searched the room.

He's looking for Octavia, Lottie realized with a sinking heart. She stood, grateful for the excuse to escape Catriona's confusing fixation on William's valet.

"Captain Hillington?" Lottie called after him as he neared the door. Heat flushed her cheeks as she recalled, unintentionally, the truth she had learned about his heritage. Thankfully, he was nothing like his misogynistic biological father.

The young man paused, dipping his head to her politely. He was remarkably shy for a ship's captain, Lottie thought to herself. But he was kind and cared for Octavia, and that was enough for her.

"I have news of Octavia," she whispered, drawing him aside from the crowd at the table.

He brightened considerably. "Is she alright? I haven't seen her all morning. We were going to walk about the gardens—"

"She received news that her father's health worsened," Lottie lied quickly, swallowing hard. "She says... she says to tell you..." She paused, wondering if she should truly break off their engagement. They seemed to genuinely care for each other, and if anyone deserved happiness, surely it was Octavia.

"She left?" Captain Hillington's hopeful expression faded, and he withdrew a small ring from his pocket. "But... my mother finally agreed to accept her."

Lottie's stomach lurched. Oh no. No, no, no, Octavia, I should never have sent you away!

Before she could stop him, Captain Hillington turned and left, closing the door firmly behind him. Clutching her skirts, she turned back to the room, desperately wishing she could find a way to contact Octavia. If Thomas had returned, perhaps he could set out immediately and retrieve her again—

Her spiraling thoughts slowed, and her neck prickled. A quick search revealed that Catriona was glaring at her over the rim of her teacup. The young woman took a tiny sip, and Lottie had never seen such a simple gesture look so menacing.

"Miss Catriona, might I have a word?" Mr. de Lacy leaned over the back of her chair and spoke quietly to her, her dark curls brushing his shoulder.

Catriona set the teacup down, still glaring at Lottie, but she nodded and rose to her feet. Mr. de Lacy helped her with her chair before leading her to the side of the room. Lottie edged closer, pretending not to listen as she watched from the corner of her eye. Could Catriona have something to do with the murders? It seemed unlikely, but that gaze of hers was certainly frightening.

"Miss Catriona, have you ever heard your brother, Lord Campbell, speak about Mr. Farraday—" Mr. de Lacy began, but Catriona cut him off, looking around quickly.

"Do you hear that?" she asked, her head turning so quickly that her dark hair flipped over her shoulder.

"Pardon?" Mr. de Lacy touched her arm as if trying to draw her attention.

Lottie watched, dread tickling her spine. Something wasn't right.

"Birds," Catriona whispered, her gaze finally landing on the magistrate. "I can hear birds..." she swayed and, as if to catch herself, she pressed her hands to Mr. de Lacy's chest.

Lottie watched in horror as Catriona's eyes rolled up, her head tipped back, and she collapsed against Mr. de Lacy.

He wrapped his arms around her waist, catching her as she fell. "Miss Catriona!" he shouted, eyes wide with alarm.

The guests gasped.

Catriona began to tremble violently, and her eyes rolled as her hands clutched Mr. de Lacy's coat.

"The doctor!" Mr. de Lacy shouted, holding her tighter as she jerked. "Someone call for the doctor!"

"What's happening?" Lottie gasped, falling to her knees beside them, unsure what to do but feeling a desperate urge to help.

The convulsions faded and Catriona's head fell back limply. Foam sparkled on her lips.

Mr. de Lacy looked up at Lottie, his mouth gaped in horror. "She's been poisoned."

***Hey guys!

Ooo, there's a lot going on now that we're nearing the end! What do you think of the clues and information from the suspects so far? Any guesses about who is the killer?

Brace yourselves, we only have about 5-6 chapters left!

Mr. de Lacy's Antidote

L ottie stared in shock. Poisoned?

"Catriona!" Lord Campbell wailed, sagging into a chair. He was certainly no help in a crisis, Lottie thought.

The doctor pushed his way into the room, shooing the guests aside. He knelt beside the unconscious woman and felt her wrist.

Thank heavens William asked him to stay and look after Fidelia the past week, Lottie thought, clutching her skirt to hide her shaking hands.

"Is she dead?" Mr. de Lacy asked. Lottie had never seen him look afraid before. It was unnerving to see him appear so... human.

The doctor shook his head slowly. "She's still alive. Quickly, take her to the family sitting room," he ordered.

Lord Campbell sat bolt-upright at the news, the color draining from his cheeks. "Still alive? There's hope for her?"

Mr. de Lacy nodded, scooping the woman up and pushing through the crowd of guests. Lottie, the Earl, and the countess all followed behind.

Lord Campbell pushed ahead to block Mr. de Lacy. "I should be the one to carry her," he said, reaching for her. "She's my sister, after all. It isn't proper for you—"

One glare from Mr. de Lacy silenced the cowardly Lord and he stepped aside, meek as a kitten.

"What happened?" the doctor asked, panting as he struggled to keep up with Mr. de Lacy's long legs.

"She's been poisoned. Deadly nightshade, I think," Mr. de Lacy said.

"How can you be sure?" the doctor huffed and wiped his brow. "It could have been any number of poisons."

"Miss Catriona said she could hear birds just before she collapsed. Such auditory hallucinations are a trademark of deadly nightshade," Mr. de Lacy explained. At last, they reached the sitting room and one of the servants rushed to open the door and light the fire.

Mr. de Lacy set the unconscious woman on the settee and stepped aside so the doctor could work. "I must ask the men to leave," the doctor ordered. The Earl and the male servants obeyed, but Mr. de Lacy and Lord Campbell refused to move.

"Can she be saved?" the countess asked. She was deadly pale and her normally well-kempt appearance was now frazzled. Lottie wondered if the sight was bringing back memories of when William had been struck over the head the year before. She wrapped a comforting around her adopted mother's shoulders.

The doctor shrugged. "The fact that she is still alive means she must have only taken a minuscule amount. She may live... or may not. Now it in the hands of the Lord in Heaven."

"Have you any Calabar bean?" Mr. de Lacy asked quietly, staring at Catriona's pale, unmoving form.

The doctor removed his glasses to clean them, blinking in confusion. "Yes, in my medical kit in my room. I use it in an elixir to treat eye irritation, but the bean is also poisonous."

"Not as an extract in small enough doses," Mr. de Lacy knelt beside Catriona and wiped the foam from her lips. "I've seen it used to counteract deadly nightshade poisoning before."

"Worth a shot, I suppose," the doctor muttered. "She could die any moment as it is." A servant was sent to fetch the medical kit and the doctor ushered everyone but Mr. de Lacy and Lord Campbell from the room.

Lottie cast one last look at Catriona as she left. Who would try to kill her, and why?

*** It was several hours before the men finally reemerged from the sitting room to announce that some color had returned to Catriona's lips, but she was still unconscious.

"How could this have happened?" the countess asked weakly. The earl patted her hand comfortingly.

"May I have a word, Mr. de Lacy?" Lottie said in a low voice, gesturing for the man to follow her further down the hallway.

He looked tired, but his brow furrowed as if he were puzzling over the situation.

Lottie had rolled the memories of that morning over and over in her mind for the duration of the treatment. Once they were far enough to avoid anyone overhearing, Lottie whispered, "It was in her teacup. I saw the liquid inside swirling as if something had fallen in."

Mr. de Lacy nodded slowly. "When was this?"

"Just after Lord Campbell and Captain Hillington bumped into her chair. Could either of them have dropped something in during the confusion?"

After a long moment, Mr. de Lacy ran a hand through his blond hair and closed his eyes. "Lord Campbell was quite distressed over his sister's condition. I doubt it could have been him. I have investigated Captain Hillington for the other two murders and he has had no motive or opportunity. It would be strange for him to suddenly resort to such a drastic action now."

"It must have been someone from the other side of the table, then," Lottie said, nibbling her thumbnail. How she wished she hadn't lost her notebook. She needed to write everything down to keep her thoughts straight.

Before Mr. de Lacy could respond, footsteps pounded down the hallway.

Lottie looked up and smiled in relief at the sight of Thomas. He was dirty and disheveled, still wearing his traveling cloak, but he was finally back.

Her smile faded when she saw how pale he appeared. Eyes wide, he grabbed her shoulder. "Is it true? Is Catriona dead?" is desperation shocked Lottie into silence.

"She's still alive," Mr. de Lacy said, removing a handkerchief to wipe his brow wearily. "But she's quite ill. She has not awoken yet."

Thomas released a breath slowly, his hand dropping from Lottie's shoulder. Eyes staring blankly ahead, he moved toward the door.

Mr. de Lacy caught his arm. "I must warn you, Thomas," he said, his voice low enough that Lottie had to strain to hear. "It will be quite shocking to see her in this state. Perhaps you should wait."

Thomas shoved the man aside and entered the room without a word to the others. Lord Campbell watched him closely, and Lottie thought she saw him smile smugly.

She followed her friend into the room and closed the door behind her, pausing at the sight.

Thomas knelt beside the settee, one of Catriona's pale hands clasped between both of his. He pressed her fingertips to his lips and stared at her face.

"Thomas?" Lottie touched his shoulder hesitantly. Unease twisted in her gut. Why were Thomas and Catriona so concerned about each other? She was the daughter of a duke and he was a stableboy temporarily acting as a valet. They shouldn't even know each other.

"She was just a child when I left," he whispered. "She begged me to stay, but I wanted to make a name for myself in the war."

Lottie blinked, confused.

"This is my fault," he closed his eyes and pressed her knuckled against his forehead. "It was my duty to protect her.

"Who is she to you?" Lottie asked, the words bitter in her mouth. Why did it hurt so much to see Thomas so concerned about another young woman?

The doctor entered the room and gestured to the door. "Miss Catriona needs to rest. Please,"

"I'm not leaving her," Thomas's voice was firm, and the doctor quickly backed away.

A lump formed in Lottie's throat and she blinked back the stinging in her eyes. She turned and left quickly. Who are you to be jealous, silly girl? She scolded herself. Thomas is free to like whoever he wants...

"Lottie?" William's voice interrupted her thoughts. He had been caring for Fidelia that morning and had missed the commotion at breakfast, but now he stood in the hallway. The others had all dispersed.

Lottie stared at him for a long moment and finally hugged him tightly, burying her head against his coat.

"What's the matter?" William asked gently as he patted her on the back. "You look as if someone just broke your heart."

"I'm so silly," Lottie whispered angrily. "Why am I getting so upset to see him so concerned about another woman?"

William's hand paused. "Thomas? Hasn't he told you who he is--?"

Lottie pulled out of the embrace and forced a smile. She waved cheerfully and hurried down the hall before her tears could fall. William called after her, but she ignored it.

Finally, she found herself in her laboratory. She needed to distract herself. Perhaps another experiment with black powder...

But she paused just inside the door, blinking in surprise. "Mr. de Lacy? What are you doing up here?"

Mr. de Lacy stood in the middle of the room, staring at the floor, his hands clasped behind his back.

Lottie swallowed hard when she realized he was staring at the rug that hid the bloodstain.

"A sudden thought occurred to me a moment ago," he said casually, but his eyes were dark when they flicked toward her. Something had changed in his demeanor since seeing Catriona poisoned. Something inside of Lottie told her that he was far more dangerous now. Far more determined to learn the truth about it all. "No one could have reached across the table to put the poison in Miss Catriona's cup. But you were right beside her."

Her nails dug into the wood of the doorway as she fought to maintain her composure. "You seem determined to blame me for every incident," she said, lifting her chin.

"They do all seem to revolve around you," he said, kicking the edge of the rug.

Lottie tensed, her eyes darting to a flash of red that appeared as the rug lifted slightly for just a moment.

"Just unlucky, I suppose," she whispered, forcing her gaze back up to his.

"Yes. You seem to lose things quite often as well," he said, gesturing to the bare floor beneath him. "A rug, for example. You can see the outline of soot where it used to be. Damage it in one of your experiments, did you?"

Refusing to answer, Lottie turned on her heel to leave. She couldn't breathe. The weight of the past couple of weeks was pressed against her chest until she struggled to draw air.

"Your maid tells me you're missing a notebook, too," Mr. de Lacy continued, following her down the stairs. "And now your dearest friend, Miss Octavia Palmer, has vanished in the night. Very strange, wouldn't you say?"

Lottie pushed against the door that led onto the castle roof and gasped as the freezing wind bit into her cheeks. Visions of Le Coquin swam in her mind. The memory of his scream as he fell. If only he had left her alone.

If she hadn't been forced to kill him to protect herself, then Mr. Farraday would never have had any leverage. She wouldn't have needed to keep so many secrets to protect William, Fidelia, and Thomas. She wouldn't be wrapped up in so many deaths.

As she stared out over the castle wall toward the ocean, Mr. de Lacy joined her. They had a clear view of the stables below and the lawn leading up to the forest on the east side of the castle. The barren trees were shrouded in thick fog rolling in from the ocean beyond.

Mr. de Lacy was silent for a moment, then asked suddenly, "has there always been two manure piles behind the stables?"

But Lottie didn't hear his strange change of subject. Instead, her attention was fixed on a man standing at the edge of the forest. He wore a long cloak and a top hat, the fog swirling around his feet. He was too far away to see his distinct features... but he was the right height and thin as a scarecrow.

"Mr. Farraday," she breathed. Before Mr. de Lacy could stop her, she turned and fled down the stairs.

She was going to catch this ghost once and for all.

***Hey guys!

Any guesses as to the mysterious relationship between Thomas and Catriona? Who do you think could have poisoned her? I'd love to hear your thoughts!

P.S. The Calabar bean, originally from Africa, is usually used as a poison, but also has some unique properties that are still used in medicine today! And it really is used as an antidote to deadly nightshade poisoning! Cool stuff. Thanks for coming to my TED talk.

Attacked In The Woods

Thomas stared at Catriona, counting each breath as her stomach rose and fell unevenly. She had been a buck-toothed kid of eleven or twelve when he had left six years before. Now she was a grown woman.

The door creaked behind him, but Thomas didn't look up.

"You haven't told Lottie who you really are, have you?" William asked.

Thomas sighed and finally set Catriona's hand back on the settee. He scrubbed at his face, willing away the exhaustion. "This is who I am now. That boy who abandoned Catriona died in the war."

William thought for a moment before sitting across from the Scotsman. "Several men have asked me for Lottie's hand this season. I cannot keep them off any longer. Sooner or later... she will marry."

The words made Thomas's heart ache and he avoided William's gaze.

William sighed. "If you have any hope of stopping that, you had best tell her the truth. She was quite distressed just a moment ago. It seems she doesn't suspect the true nature of your relationship with Catriona."

Thomas nodded slowly. Perhaps it was time to tell Lottie the truth. Even if she wouldn't have him… he could no longer deny the feelings that grew stronger each day.

***Just as Thomas began his search, he spotted Lottie from a window in the hallway. She was outside, without a cloak in spite of the snowflakes that were drifting from the sky.

His shoulders tensed. She seemed to be in a trance of some sort, striding purposefully towards the line of trees.

Thomas followed her gaze. "Och, nay," he whispered. A cloak swirled through the fog as a man turned, leading the way deeper into the forest. And Lottie followed right behind.

"William!" he shouted over his shoulder.

***Snow crunched beneath Lottie's leather boots as she followed the man's footsteps. The fog muted all sounds, and her heartbeat pounded in her ears. He was real. How could he still be alive? She had seen his dead body!

The trees loomed out of the fog and Lottie had to readjust with each step. It wasn't long before she realized she was hopelessly lost. She paused, listening for any sounds.

"Where is it?" a man's gravelly voice asked through the white clouds surrounding her. The voice was familiar, but they spoke roughly as if trying to disguise themselves. But she knew one thing for certain. It wasn't Mr. Farraday.

Lottie spun, reaching for her knife, only to remember too late that she had given it to Octavia.

"Who are you?" she shouted back, turning in circles. "What do you want? Why are you doing this to me?"

"If you won't give it to me... I suppose I'll just have to take it from your corpse," the voice sounded to her left and she twisted to face it, gasping for breath.

"Lottie!" Thomas's shout pierced the fog as footsteps rushed at her from two sides.

Thomas wrapped an arm around her waist, spinning her to the side.

A blade hissed through the air behind her, slicing through one of her blond curls as she turned.

Thomas held her tightly against his chest and spun them around again as their attacker swiped again, but they turned too far and Lottie's back collided against the coarse bark of a tree.

"Watch out!" Lottie cried, peering under Thomas's arm as the man in the cloak flipped the knife over in his hand and swung.

With nowhere to go, Thomas pressed Lottie against the tree, curling his body around hers to protect her.

***

The blade slashed Thomas's shoulder and down across to his hip.

He cried out, arching in pain. Hot blood ran down his back.

"Thomas!" Lottie screamed. She grabbed his shirt and tried to push him out of the way, but he held her tighter.

"Don't," he hissed, pressing her face against his chest and wrapping his other arm around her shoulders.

The man in the cloak laughed and slashed again. Pain seared across Thomas's ribs and his knees buckled. He fell, dragging Lottie down with him into the snow.

"Thomas! Let go, he'll kill you!" she sobbed, trying to pull away from him.

As his brain grew fuzzy with the pain, he pressed her down, covering her as best he could.

The man kicked at her, but the blow landed on Thomas's side. He grunted, his grip on her loosening.

"Stop it!" Lottie screamed. "Please, don't hurt him!"

The man drew back the bloody knife, preparing to stab down.

"Lottie!" William's voice echoed through the fog.

The man jerked around, his face hidden behind a black cloth, and hissed in annoyance.

He vanished into the mist, his cloak swirling after him.

Thomas's remaining strength finally gave out and his head sagged against hers, his hands falling away from her shoulders.

***Lottie rolled Thomas off of her, instantly regretting it when he winced as the snow bit into his cuts.

"No," she whispered, pulling him into her lap. Dark blood stained the snow around him as she grabbed his face. "No, no, no, you—keep your eyes open—Thomas, no—"

His eyes opened for a moment and stared blearily up at her. His lips twitched. "Pretty potato," he muttered, then his eyes closed again.

Lottie moaned and tapped his face. "Wake up. Wake up!" Desperate, she pressed her lips to his to shock him awake.

Nothing. Tears streaming down her cheeks, she pressed her forehead to his. Foolish, foolish man!

Voices echoed around them in the fog and she looked up. The sounds were moving past her as if they were lost in the trees.

She pulled Thomas against her chest, resting his head on her shoulder, and she tried to press her hands over the cuts, but they were too long. "Help!" she sobbed, holding him tighter. "Someone, please help him."

"Lottie?" William called again, closer this time.

Unable to form a coherent word, Lottie just shouted as blood oozed out between her fingers.

William and several servants with torches emerged from the mist and Lottie sobbed harder, burying her face against Thomas's neck. "Hold on," she whispered in his ear. "You'll be okay."

***Lottie refused to leave Thomas's side as the servants carried him back to the castle. Blood soaked the front of her blue dress, turning it crimson, and it stained her hands and the tips of her hair. But she couldn't leave him.

The servants laid him facedown on the floor in the kitchen, which was situated just inside the servant's entrance, while a maid ran to fetch the doctor.

"What happened?" William asked, removing his coat and pressing it over the long cuts on the man's back.

"I saw Mr. Farraday. Or... someone pretending to be him," Lottie shook her head, unable to remember clearly. It was all so blurry now. She couldn't think straight. "I followed him into the forest, and he attacked. Thomas..."

She knelt beside his head, brushing back his dark hair from his brow. "He protected me. Foolish man."

William sighed and shook his head.

The doctor arrived with Fidelia, who froze at the sight of the blood.

William's hands tightened around the coat he pressed to Thomas's back. "Someone get her out of here," he ordered.

Fidelia shook her head. "I'm staying," she snapped.

"Fidelia, your health—" William started, but a flash of Fidelia's green eyes silenced him.

The doctor swallowed hard at the sight of Thomas's back. "The ladies should leave—"

"No," Lottie and Fidelia said simultaneously. Cowed by their combined ferocity, the doctor raised his hand in submission and set about cutting away the back of Thomas's shirt.

Lottie winced as shreds of blood-soaked cloth were pulled away from his skin.

Once his back was entirely exposed, Lottie gasped and covered her mouth. His back was covered in scars. Two round, raised scars donned his left shoulder blade, and other long lines traced over his ribs, spine, and shoulders.

"What happened to him?" Lottie asked, touching one of the circular scars.

"Wounds from the war," William whispered. "Those are from being shot."

"The long ones are from cuts," the doctor agreed, cleaning the fresh wounds. "Bayonets, most likely."

She shook her head, smoothing the puckered skin with her thumb. "Why didn't he tell me? He never said anything about the war."

"He came back a broken man," William said, gathering up the shredded shirt. "Most of the men in his battalion didn't make it. Like most survivors... the scars run deeper than his skin."

"Pray he stays unconscious. I don't have time to give him laudanum to numb the pain," the doctor said as he prepared to stitch the cuts closed.

Lottie took Thomas's hand, holding it tightly as the doctor sewed the skin back together. By the time he moved to the second gash, she had to close her eyes. She couldn't bear to see her gentle Scotsman like this.

***After the operation was complete, the doctor sent Lottie away, saying he was worried she would be sick. William promised to stay beside him and Fidelia guided Lottie away.

A servant met them in the hallway. "Lady Greyville! Mr. de Lacy has—"

Fidelia cut them off, eyeing Lottie sideways, as if concerned that the man's name would cause more distress to her younger sister.

"I must deal with this," Fidelia said, taking Lottie's hand. "Will you be alright?"

Lottie stared ahead, the crusted blood on her hands cracking as she balled them into fists. "Can I have Father's pistol? I... I would feel better if I could borrow it for protection."

Fidelia nodded and removed the pistol from her pocket. After Lottie reassured her sister she would be alright, Fidelia hurried after the servant.

Once they were gone, Lottie set her jaw. That man had hurt Thomas. She would make him pay with his life.

***

Once Lottie had changed into a clean dress and donned a thick cloak, she snuck out the servant's entrance and down to the stables.

There was a commotion behind the stables, but Lottie ignored it once she heard Mr. de Lacy shouting. She didn't have time to worry about his accusations. She needed to catch up with Thomas's attacker before his trail was lost to the falling snow.

She snuck around to the front of the stable and ordered the new stableboy to saddle a horse for her. Since Esquire was still injured from the morning he had fallen in the snow and thrown Thomas, she rode one of the smaller mares out of the stable and into the forest before anyone else noticed she was gone.

Once in the trees, Lottie followed the trail of blood back to the scene of the attack, then followed the footprints further into the woods. For an hour, Lottie followed the trail, her hope of catching the man slowly vanishing as gathering snow covered the footprints.

At last, the trail disappeared completely and Lottie growled, leaning over the saddle to press her forehead against the horse's neck. "What am I going to do?" she whispered, refusing to cry again. She couldn't let the killer continue hurting the people around her. She had to stop him.

As if bored, the horse lumbered forward through the trees along a game path and, out of ideas, Lottie let the mare have her head. The trees eventually gave way to farmland, and they continued on until she could smell the ocean. They topped a small rise and Lottie drew the horse to a stop, gazing down at the jagged rocks that led to the beach. The wind from the ocean had blown the fresh snow away, leading the sharp black stones clear.

A fluttering motion caught her attention and Lottie dismounted, stepping carefully across the sharp rocks.

As she drew close enough, she snatched up a scrap of cloth. It was a long, grey piece... stained with crimson.

She stared at the fabric for a long time, trying to remember why it seemed so familiar...

"Mr. Farraday's coat," she whispered, clutching the scrap tighter in her hand. That day on the beach when she had found his body, his grey coat had lain in tatters around him. She had thought it was from the waves, but could it have been shredded by someone dragging his body across these rocks on their way to dump it into the ocean?

More fluttering drew her attention to another scrap. Then another. She followed the trail until, about halfway across the rock field, she found another. But this one was different. Instead of grey stained with blood, it was a yellow and brown plaid.

Heart pounding, she examined it again. It was also stained with blood. The wind howled in her ears, whipping her hair about her face. She had seen this yellow and brown plaid before... on a pair of trousers missing a portion on the knee. Finally, she pressed the cloth to her stomach. "Thomas... what have you done?"

***Hey guys!

This was quite the packed chapter! What did you think of the attack in the woods? Too dramatic?

And what do you think of the big reveal about Thomas at the end? I'd love to hear your thoughts!

If you liked this chapter, please be sure to comment and vote!

Truth Revealed

L ottie tucked the scrap of Thomas's trousers into her pocket and rode quickly back to the castle. She needed to hear the truth for herself. She refused to believe the evidence that he had... he had...

"Foolish man," she whispered, the blowing snow freezing the tears on her cheeks.

Once at the castle, Lottie slid from the saddle and slapped the reins into the stableboy's hand and ignored his shouts that the magistrate had found something awful.

Her boots slipped on the polished floors in the foyer as she ran through the front doors and towards the kitchen. But before she could enter the hallway down to the lower level, two men with rifles barred her way.

"Please come with us, Miss Lottie," one said, gesturing with his gun.

"Get out of my way," Lottie ordered, lifting her chin. "I am the charge of Lord Greyville, how dare you try to block me in my own home?"

The man growled and grabbed her by the upper arm.

"Let go of me!" Lottie shouted, reaching for her father's pistol in her pocket.

The man's companion grabbed her other arm before she could draw the gun and hauled her up the stairs. She fought against them, their hands on her arms making her nauseous with memories of Edmund and Le Coquin. She howled in frustration but they dragged her on until, at last, they reached the drawing room.

They pushed the door open and pulled her roughly inside. Her family and all the guests had gathered, sitting nervously as Mr. de Lacy paced the room.

Fidelia shot to her feet at the sight of Lottie's captors. "Unhand my sister," she growled, reaching into her pocket as if forgetting that she had loaned the gun to Lottie.

"We've brought the culprit, sir," one of the men said, ignoring Fidelia's demands and nodding to Mr. de Lacy.

"Let her go," William demanded, wrapping an arm around his wife's waist protectively.

The magistrate flicked his fingers and the men finally released Lottie's arms. She shoved them aside, her breath ragged as she fought to keep her memories in check. She wasn't at the abandoned mill with Le Coquin. She wasn't there. But she wasn't safe, either.

"What's the meaning of this?" she marched up to Mr. de Lacy and glared at him, but she faltered as his eyes flashed.

Edmund. Why did he have to look so much like Edmund? She blinked, trying to force the memories away.

"We found Mr. Farraday," the magistrate replied coolly, his face a mask of calm that set Lottie's teeth on edge. "Or what's left of him, at least."

The air froze in her lungs. She had to step back. "Where?"

"Behind the stables. It seems someone tried to bury him, but the ground was too frozen. They settled for covering his body with half of the manure pile. It hid the stench well enough, but it was sloppy work, I must say," Mr. de Lacy spoke lightly as if simply discussing the weather during tea and not a gruesome murder.

The manure pile. Lottie dropped her gaze to the floor. She had noticed the separate pile several nights before, but Thomas had dismissed it and she hadn't spared it another thought.

"Would you care to explain this?" Mr. de Lacy drew a notebook out of his coat's inner pocket, waving it back and forth through the air languidly.

With trembling fingers, Lottie reached for it. "That's my notebook. W-where did you find it?"

"Pinned beneath Mr. Farraday's body."

The book slipped through her fingers and fell to the floor, landing open.

Lottie stared at it, drawing long, slow breaths to calm her racing heart. "I... I lost it the day he disappeared. But I swear, I had nothing to do with—"

"I have grown tired of your lies, Miss Lottie," Mr. de Lacy snapped, finally dropping his calm exterior. "Tell me the truth." His blue eyes blazed down at her. "Now!"

"De Lacy!" William protested, but the guard moved to stand before him, his gun gripped tightly. William glared at the man and Lottie saw his hand tighten around Fidelia. She couldn't allow them to get involved.

"Leave them alone," she whispered, shaking her head.

"Only if you tell me the truth," Mr. de Lacy responded.

"I didn't do it," she backed up a step.

He followed, matching her pace. "Several people witnessed Mr. Farraday speaking to you at the ball the night before the house party began. They said you grew quite distressed. Is that when he first tried to blackmail you?"

She swallowed hard and nodded. "He was going to ruin me. Ruin everything."

"And when he came to the house party, you lured him up to your laboratory and killed him. Several of the servants stated that a spear resided in that room until very recently. Around the time Mr. Farraday disappeared, to be exact. The tip of that same spear was also found with the body," his voice was low but confident.

The guests gasped. Lady Hillington pressed a hand to her chest. Sir Roland muttered under his breath about "see what happens to young ladies who meddle in men's work?" and Lord Campbell nodded vigorously in agreement.

"I didn't kill him," she repeated, still stepping back.

"That same night, Mrs. Ashdown witnessed you running through the castle halls, blood on your hands, pale as a ghost. She told me about it the night before she died. That's why you killed her, isn't it? Because she was trying to expose you," Mr. de Lacy's eyes narrowed. "I have interrogated everyone in the castle. No one else can account for your whereabouts that night."

Lottie shook her head desperately. That wasn't Mr. Farraday's blood. It was Octavia's. She had stopped the knife that Lottie had swung while caught in her nightmares. The only other person who knew where she had been that night was Thomas, but he was lying unconscious in the kitchen, struggling to stay alive.

"Your laboratory is missing a rug. You rolled Mr. Farraday's body in it so you could get it out of the castle without anyone knowing. But you couldn't get him very far, so you buried him in the manure pile, didn't you?" his voice rose and he loomed over her. "Didn't you?"

She tripped on the hem of her dress and landed hard on her hip. Fidelia cried out, but William held her back. The countess whimpered and buried her head in the Earl's shoulder. He looked as if he were about to protest, but the other guard stepped in front of him. In this situation, the Magistrate outranked the Earl. Several people had been killed and one was on death's doorstep, after all.

"Did the notebook fall out of your pocket while moving him? Is that why you never noticed it?" Mr. de Lacy pressed. "After you buried the body, you returned to the castle and tried to clean up the evidence, but you were muddy and smelled of manure. You left a mark of it on the floor in your bedroom. I discovered it during my search this evening."

Lottie could only shake her head again. She remembered clearly now. The notebook had flown from her hands when she tripped over Mr. Farraday's body on the beach, and in her haste to leave, she had forgotten it in the sand.

But she couldn't tell him the truth. Now that she knew Thomas was involved, she couldn't bear to put him in danger.

The door creaked open, and everyone looked up to see Thomas leaning heavily on the frame. He had draped a coat over the shredded remains of his shirt, which was still bloody.

His face pale, he pushed away from the frame and stepped between Mr. de Lacy and Lottie, who still sat numbly on the floor.

"She had nothing to do with it," Thomas said quietly, his voice hoarse. He paused to look back at her, his eyes sorrowful. He stared at her for a long moment before he nodded and faced Mr. de Lacy again. "It was me. I killed Mr. Farraday."

For The Love Of Lottie

T homas winced as Lottie gasped behind him.

Mr. de Lacy narrowed his eyes. "You? The valet?"

Thomas dropped his gaze and nodded. "I knew Mr. Farraday was causing Miss Lottie great distress and could no longer stand by as he tormented her."

"No!" Lottie pushed to her feet and clutched his hand. "Stop, why are you doing this—"

He pulled away, biting his cheek as the movement tugged at his stitches. He could feel the intrigued gazes of the guests piercing into them. He couldn't let them think that there was something improper between him and Lottie.

"Please compose yourself, Miss Lottie," he whispered, stepping further away.

"What happened?" Mr. de Lacy asked, raising a brow as if he wasn't quite convinced.

Thomas forced his gaze away from Lottie. He would lose his courage if he looked into her tear-filled eyes. "I followed Mr. Farraday up to the laboratory and... and pushed him onto the spear."

Mr. de Lacy clasped his hands behind his back. "How did you move the body?"

"I rolled him in the rug and dragged him onto the parapets. I knew Miss Lottie had constructed a pulley system to transport her supplies up the walls, and I used it to lower his body down. I had access to the stables and it was easy to bury him in the manure pile."

The guests whispered amongst themselves. Thomas spared a glance at William, who was staring at him in horror.

"But that doesn't explain the blood on Miss Lottie's hands or the smear of mud and manure in her room," Mr. de Lacy protested.

Thomas dipped his head apologetically to William. "Miss Lottie had accidentally cut the hand of her friend, Miss Palmer, during the early morning hours. She was running to fetch bandages."

"Miss Palmer has disappeared," Mr. de Lacy's lip twitched as if pleased to have caught Lottie in Thomas's lie.

"The maid, Sally, witnessed it," Thomas said.

After a long pause, Mr. de Lacy gestured to one of his men. "Find the maid. We shall see if she corroborates this." The man hurried off and the magistrate gestured to Thomas to continue.

"Miss Lottie has been out to the stables many times over the past two weeks for riding lessons. She could have easily gotten the mud on her clothes and left a trace in her room."

The guests nodded as if the explanation made sense, but Mr. de Lacy remained skeptical. "What of Mrs. Ashdown?"

Thomas blinked. He hadn't thought that far ahead.

"Thomas, don't do this," Lottie begged, reaching for him again.

William left Fidelia's side and snatched Lottie's hand, pulling her back. "Be quiet," he ordered her, eyes hard as he glared at Thomas.

"But he didn't—" Lottie protested.

"Silence!" William's voice thundered, stunning his sister-in-law so much that she shrank back.

Thomas clenched his hands into fists. He opened his mouth to protest, but finally, he turned away. He couldn't show concern for her. It would only sully her reputation more. "I overheard Mrs. Ashdown's conversation with ye the night she died. I knew she was trying to cast suspicion onto Miss Lottie, so... so I killed her, too."

Mr. de Lacy finally nodded. "You have convinced me, Mr. Hawthorne. Pardon me, Lord Greyville, but I shall require the use of the castle dungeon until I can transport this murderer to the prison in Sunderland once the storm clears." He gestured to the remaining guards. "Seize him."

"No!" Lottie cried, pushing past William. She grabbed Thomas's arm, her eyes pleading with him as she shook her head. "No, don't let them do this—"

The guards seized his arms, pulling him away. The movements strained his stitches and fresh blood trickled down his back. He clenched his jaw, seething at the pain.

"Let go of him!" Lottie shouted, trying to shove them aside, but William wrapped his arms around her waist and dragged her back.

As he was dragged from the room, he cast one final glance back at his Lottie. The remaining pins in her golden hair flew loose as she struggled against William, who held her tightly.

Fidelia stared in horror, finally rising to help her husband contain the struggling young woman. At last, Lottie's legs gave out and she fell to her knees, tears tracking down her cheeks as she stared hopelessly after Thomas.

Forgive me, wee lassie.

*** "He's innocent!" Lottie shouted as William pushed her into the family's sitting room. Fidelia followed closely behind, shutting the door tightly.

William towered over her, breathing hard. He stamped his cane against the floor. "Have you no shame, Lottie?"

"William," Fidelia cautioned, but William held up his hand to stop her.

"I have let her run wild for long enough," he said. Turning back to Lottie, he gestured to the door. "The circumstances of these murders, Mr. Farraday's attempt to blackmail... Thomas's guilt. You knew all of this, and yet you hid it from us? You even throw yourself at the murderer without a shred of propriety, just like you did with Ed—"

Lottie rounded on him until they were nose to nose. "Just like I did with Edmund?" she growled.

Fidelia laid a hand on his shoulder. "You've gone too far, my love."

William sighed and his shoulders sagged. "I didn't mean it," he rubbed a hand wearily against his brow. "Forgive me, Lottie. I know what happened with Edmund was not your fault. I spoke out of anger."

The words still burned in Lottie's mind in spite of his apology. "Thomas is innocent. We hid this from you to protect you. But now he's foolishly gone and falsely confessed to the murders—"

"Why would he do something like that?" William threw his hand into the air. "If he didn't do it, why would he confess—"

Lottie closed her eyes tightly. "I don't know why he did it... but I know he's innocent. Think about it, William. He was just attacked in the woods by the real killer while trying to protect me." She grasped her brother-in-law's hand desperately. "He wasn't even in the castle when Catriona was poisoned, and he never said anything to explain how Miss Wilde and Lord Campbell both saw someone dressed as Mr. Farraday leaving the castle."

William's gaze faltered. "He would never have harmed Catriona," he agreed slowly.

"Besides," Lottie added, "I found Mr. Farraday's body on the beach at sunrise that day. I ran straight to the stables to get Thomas. There is no way Thomas could have returned to the beach, moved the body to the castle and bury it in the manure pile, then remove all evidence of it by the time I found him. When we returned to the beach, the body was gone... along with my notebook that I dropped in my haste."

Fidelia wrapped a hand around William's arm and nodded. "She's right, husband. There are too many things that don't fit."

William thought for a moment, twisting the cane between his fingers. "I will speak to Thomas about this, but Lottie... I am ordering you to stay out of this from now on."

*** Thomas sat on the floor of the castle's dungeon, his back pressed against the freezing stone wall. At least it numbed the searing pain from his wounds.

After escorting him to the dungeon, Mr. de Lacy had left a single guard to watch over him, but he had fallen asleep not long after.

His mind drifted to Lottie, remembering the way she had reached for him so desperately. Where was she now? Was she alright?

"I knew you were foolish," William's voice echoed in the stone room as he emerged from the darkness, "but I never knew you were a love-struck idiot."

Thomas's lips twitched. "Love-struck, eh?"

William glanced at the sleeping guard, who was hunched over an empty bottle of whiskey, and rolled his eyes. He kicked a stool over to the bars and sat. "That is the only explanation I could come up with for why you would do something so utterly idiotic. You love her, don't you?"

Thomas swallowed hard and held his friend's gaze. He had told enough lies for one day... at least he could speak the truth now. "Aye. With all my soul."

William's shoulders sagged and he rubbed at his beard. "You realize that by confessing to these murders, you have separated yourself from her forever?"

Thomas nodded, his breath fogging the air between them. "But at least she will be safe. Mr. de Lacy could never find an alibi for Lottie during the time of the murders... because she was always with me," he paused. "Alone."

William drew a sharp breath. He clenched fists and struck one against his leg. "She would be proven innocent, but her reputation would be ruined."

Shoulder's sagging, Thomas swallowed hard. "I never intended to harm her reputation. I feared for her safety and... and thus I justified being alone with her to guard her."

Cheeks red, William narrowed his eyes angrily. "For the moment I will ignore your utter disregard for propriety towards my sister-in-law. Now, tell me what really happened."

As the guard slept on, Thomas relayed how, after returning Lottie to the castle the night Mr. Farraday tried to blackmail her, Thomas had gone up to the laboratory to confront him. Instead, he found the man dead—impaled on the spear. Suspecting that it had been done to frame Lottie, he had dragged the body down the stairs and used the pulley system to transport it to the ground.

Then he used Esquire to take the body to the ocean, but the horse had tripped in the snow and cut his leg near the beach, so Thomas had dragged the body over the rocks, falling and tearing the knee from his trousers. He threw the body into the ocean, but it had somehow washed back onto the shore where Lottie found it.

"From then on," Thomas explained, "I knew Lottie would be in grave danger. The attempt on her life today is proof that the blackmailer has been waiting for an opportunity."

William stayed silent for a moment, the cane spinning between his fingers. Finally, he raised his gaze to Thomas. "Because of your confession... I fear there is no hope for 'Thomas the stable hand.' De Lacy is out for blood. You'll be executed for this."

Thomas looked up at the bars between them. Somehow, he had convinced himself days ago that there could be a future for him and Lottie. But that was gone now. "When I returned from the war... I had no desire to live. Now, I have someone I desperately wish to survive with and yet I find myself at death's door."

"If rumors of this ever arise, it will be impossible to find Lottie a respectable husband," William groaned and covered his eyes. "I fear I must act preemptively to ensure that she is taken care of, should... should anything happen to me."

Thomas's heart ached at the thought of Lottie being married off to some man who wouldn't support her love of invention, someone who didn't understand how a man's touch filled her with nightmares of Edmund and Le Coquin... someone who would cause the light in her eyes to fade. But William was right. Without a male heir, William's estate would pass to a distant relative, no matter how he might wish to leave everything to Fidelia and Lottie.

"Unless..." William's sat forward, a gleam in his eyes.

"What are you planning?" Thomas asked, worried about the excited grin on his old friend's face. it had always spelled trouble when they were schoolboys with Edmund and Charles.

"I believe it is time to solicit the aid of Lord McCabe."

Engaged To Lord McCabe

Lottie stood in the middle of Thomas's room, looking around at the sparse furnishings and well-made bed, wondering if he was warm enough down in the dungeons. She had tried to sneak down to see him several times, but there were too many guards. After William had spoken to Thomas, he had refused to see Lottie, saying only that he would continue to investigate the matter.

"It's been two days," she whispered, trailing her fingers across the small writing desk. Two days and still no news.

The house was buzzing with activity as the servants prepared for the Earl's annual Christmas Eve Masquerade Ball, to be held that evening. The countess had attempted to cancel in light of the murders, but gossip of a murderer's arrest in Lambton Castle had only increased interest in the ball. Several ladies from the surrounding towns had already come calling, eager for gossip, despite the mounds of snow left by the blizzard.

In all the commotion, Lottie slipped away and snuck into Thomas's valet quarters, situated near William's in the east wing. Even though he had only acted as a valet for a short time, the room already smelled of leather and juniper.

Lifting the lid on the writing desk, she paused at the sight of a folded letter with Wee Lassie scrawled across the back. Hesitantly, she removed it and broke the wax seal. Perhaps it contained something that could prove his innocence.

My dearest Lottie,

Forgive me, for I find I can no longer keep these words locked inside my heart and must express them, even if it be in a letter that I know I can never deliver.

Ye once said to me that ye do not know what the word 'love' means anymore. In truth, I ken ye despise it, so I will endeavor to express my heart without it.

I shall not swear to love ye. I shall not whisper sweet words that mean nothing to ye.

Should the day come that I can be a man worthy of ye, let these be my vows to ye instead. I swear to be by yer side when the blanket of night enfolds us each evening and watch the light of sunrise shining on yer face each morning.

I swear to watch in deepest adoration as ye experiment and invent things that will change the world; to laugh with ye during the joyful times, hold ye in the sad, and work beside ye through the hard.

I swear to paint yer eyebrows on each day with only a bit of teasing, take yer hand in the quiet hours, and walk beside ye when nightmares keep ye from sleep. To change the nappies when the wee bairns come, play with them in the garden, and hold them as they cry at night.

Although I shall not say I love ye, I shall show it to ye in each action and each moment until we are both grey and old, on until we join together in heaven. Ye shall never be alone, nor shall ye ever need to wonder if my heart is true and honest, for I shall nae leave ye again.

Sincerely,

Yer Scotsman.

Lottie stumbled back a step and sank to the ground, reading the letter over again. "Oh, Thomas," she whispered as tears blurred the scrawling words. How could she have been so blind? How had she never realized how he felt for her?

She shook her head, pushing her blond curls from her face, holding the letter to her chest. She had to see him. She had to tell him—

She raised her gaze and spotted something glinting under the bed. She reached under and slid it out, the metal scraping against the wood with a hiss.

It was the breastplate that he said he would reshape for her so she could use it as protection during her experiments. True to his word, he had cut, welded, and hammered the plate until it fit perfectly over her chest and stomach. Tears finally fell, splashing onto the silvery surface. He had loved her quietly, gently, and without an expectation for anything in return... and she had never noticed.

Swiping briskly at her tears, Lottie hugged the plate and letter to her stomach, stumbling to her feet. She would save him from the dungeon, no matter the ruin it would bring to her reputation.

*** Lottie's steps slowed as she neared the family's private sitting room and raised voices echoed through the hallway.

"Don't feign ignorance with me, Lord Greyville," Mr. de Lacy shouted. "I know you went to visit him just before—"

William clucked his tongue and Lottie paused at the corner, peering around to watch the confrontation.

"Careful, Mr. de Lacy," William said, his voice dripping with sarcastic concern. "It would be a shame if people heard what happened. Such negligence could cost you your position."

Mr. de Lacy's jaw worked, and he glared at William. With a jerk, he grabbed the lord's arm and pulled him close to whisper in his ear.

William smiled and flicked away Mr. de Lacy's hand. "Noted. Now, if you'll excuse me, I have a ball to prepare for... and you have a prisoner to attend to."

Mr. de Lacy ran a hand angrily through his pale hair, his nostril flaring. He spun and stalked away, hands clenched into fists.

Lottie pressed her back to the wall, holding her breath. Had something happened?

"You can come out now," William said from just around the corner. He was deceptively quiet for a man who walked with a cane.

Lottie slapped a hand over her mouth to hide her squeal. Sheepishly, she rounded the corner and grinned.

"How much did you hear?" William asked, raising a brow.

"Everything," Lottie lifted her chin.

His lips twitched. "You wouldn't be so cheerful if you had actually heard anything important," he wrapped an arm around her shoulders and guided her into the sitting room.

"Oh, Lottie," the countess smiled wearily from her chair beside Fidelia. "It's good that you've come. The seamstress has brought our dresses for the masquerade ball."

Lottie grimaced. She had no desire to attend the ball, not when Thomas was shivering in the dungeon falsely accused of murder.

"I... also have something to discuss with you about tonight's ball," William began hesitantly. "And about Thomas."

The Earl, countess, and Fidelia all paused. The hairs on the back of her neck prickled. Something felt wrong. Silently, she turned back to William.

He opened his mouth but paused, twisting the cane between his fingers. "I have invited a particularly important guest to the ball tonight."

"Who?" Lottie asked, forcing herself to stay still as suspicion churned inside her.

"Lottie..." he began again, "although I have kept it from you until now, I cannot any longer. Many men have asked me for your hand throughout the season, and, in light of the scandal, I fear that if we wait any longer, we will be unable to secure you a suitable marriage."

"Who is coming tonight?" Lottie asked, louder this time. She set her jaw and glared at him, doing her best imitation of Fidelia.

"Your fiancé," William dropped his gaze. "Lord McCabe. I have accepted his proposal on your behalf. I will announce it tonight at the ball."

The chest plate clattered to the floor, the letter fluttering down after it. Lottie searched their faces. "You... you sold me off?"

The countess rose and reached for Lottie's hand. "It's not like that, my dear, it's just that—"

"No," Lottie growled, pulling away. "No, I refuse. How could you just marry me off to a stranger after you know what I have been through? How could you do this to me?" her voice rose.

"William," Fidelia's voice broke as she turned pleadingly to her husband. "Surely there's another way—"

"I love Thomas," Lottie's voice echoed clearly in the sitting room. The countess and earl gasped. "I will not be wed to any man but him."

William's cheeks heated and he glanced at the door as if ensuring it was closed. Finally, he laid a heavy hand on her shoulder. "Listen to me, Lottie," his blue eyes bored into hers. "You must give up any hope of a future with Thomas the stable hand. That is no longer possible."

His words felt like a strike to her gut. "Has something happened to Thomas?" she asked quietly.

Fidelia swallowed hard and nodded. "Mr. de Lacy has taken Thomas to the prison in Sunderland. He will be tried the day after tomorrow."

"But there's not enough proof—" Lottie protested, panic rising in her chest as she struggled to breathe.

"Mr. de Lacy seems confident," William interrupted. "He assures me that, once convicted, Thomas will be hanged immediately."

"No!" Lottie shouted, running toward the door.

William caught her arm and spun her around. "It's too late. He's already gone. All we can do now is plan for your future."

She shoved away, gathering up the chest plate and letter. She was too furious for tears. This couldn't be the end. She refused. "How could you?" she whispered.

Turning, she fled from the room.

*** Lottie sat on the floor in her room with her knees pulled up to her chest, staring at the letter and breastplate.

Thomas was gone.

She had searched for him in the dungeon only to find it entirely empty. The guards had left the castle as well, but Mr. de Lacy remained behind for the ball.

How could William simply marry her off to a stranger as easily as selling a horse at market? How could they expect her to meekly obey, knowing that Thomas was going to be executed in two days?

"Miss?" Sally entered the darkened room with a large box. "I've come to dress you for the ball."

"I'm not going," Lottie said, her voice flat. She had to think of a way to save Thomas.

Sally silently lit several candles and prepared the dress. It was a renaissance style, with a red bodice and underskirt and black overskirt. She set out a matching mask, adorned with black feathers around the rim.

"Oh," Sally said, hesitantly crouching beside Lottie. "Mr. de Lacy asked that I deliver this to you," she drew Lottie's notebook from her pocket. She helped Lottie to the vanity and set about styling her hair.

Lottie turned the notebook over in her hands. Why did the blackmailer take it from the beach and hide it with the body?

"Bloody sand..." she muttered to herself, her hands stilling.

"Pardon?" Sally leaned over her shoulder to hear better.

"Why was there bloody sand in both Octavia's and Lady Hillington's rooms? And the mud in mine...?" she stared hard at the notebook as Sally shrugged and went back to brushing Lottie's hair.

The blackmailer was looking for something. But he only searched for it after he took my notebook and buried the body.

She slapped her hand on the vanity, making Sally jump. "The notebook!" Lottie pushed to her feet and grabbed the maid's shoulders, giving them a little shake. "The blackmailer was looking for the notebook. Not mine, but Mr. Farraday's, the one that supposedly held so much evidence against us all. The blackmailer never had it, that's why he never followed through with his threats to expose me! He knew someone else must have the real notebook!"

Sally gawked, her brown eyes wide. "What are you going on about, miss?"

Lottie grinned, her gaze falling on the breastplate on the floor, a wild idea spinning in her head. "I know what he wants. I know how to draw him out. I can save Thomas!"

Lottie Attacked

‒‒‒

Lottie ran her fingers along the feathers rimming the mask over her eyes, gazing out across the crowded ballroom. The masquerade ball was in full force, with dazzling gowns and glittering masks flashing in the candlelight as guests mingled and danced.

"Are you ready?" she whispered over her shoulder to Sally, who stood at the edge of the ballroom, worrying the edge of her apron until the threads came loose.

"I don't like this, Miss," Sally said, "it be too dangerous! Shouldn't we just tell Lord and Lady Greyville?"

Lottie drew a deep breath to steady herself. "No," she said, remembering the way William had accused her of throwing herself shamelessly at Thomas, 'just like she had with Edmund.' Even if he mistakenly said it in a moment of anger, she didn't dare tell him her desperate plan to save her Scotsman. He would stop her for sure. "I'll be perfectly safe. Just get into position."

Sally nodded, pulling her maid's cap lower over her ears. "I heard from the other maids that Lord McCabe has already arrived. His mask is painted gold and covers his entire face."

Lottie nodded and tucked her thumbs into her fists. She had no intention of meeting her fiancé that evening.

Sally slipped through the crowd and Lottie counted in her head, knowing it would take several minutes for the young maid to get up to the laboratory and into her hiding place.

Steadying herself, Lottie pressed into the crowd. She greeted the guests as they approached her but moved on before she could be sucked into a conversation. Finally, she found Sir Roland, his face ruddy and swollen already from too many drinks.

"What, ho!" he leered, grabbing her hand.

She crinkled her nose at his fowl stench but froze before she could pull away. Just behind him stood a tall man, staring at her from behind a full-faced mask, painted in gold. White feathers arched from the top of the mask and over his hair.

They watched each other for a long moment before he stepped forward. "Miss Lottie, might I have this dance?" his deep voice rang with a perfect British accent. Lord McCabe. Even if Sally hadn't warned her, Lottie would have guessed it was him judging by the gold brocade of his waistcoat and silver cravat. An utter dandy without a thought in his head, surely.

Lottie turned away sharply and smiled at Sir Roland. "Come, Sir Roland, I believe I have already promised this dance to you."

Sir Roland sucked in his enormous potbelly and touched the side of his nose. "I knew you couldn't avoid me forever. Finally acknowledged your ardent feelings for me, eh?"

She rolled her eyes and dragged him out to the dance floor.

"Wait!" Lord McCabe called after her but she ignored him.

She danced for several long minutes with the odious Sir Roland before she gathered her courage. Oh, how she missed the gossip-mongering skills of Octavia and Mrs. Ashdown. If only they were here, it would have been so much easier to spread the rumor that would draw out the real killer.

"Did you hear?" she said with a hint of mischief as she leaned closer. "Mr. Farraday's notebook has been found."

Sir Roland froze in the middle of the floor, his face paling. "Y-you don't say...? Who could have found it?"

Lottie smiled and touched the side of her nose, imitating his signature motion. "I did, of course. But don't tell the others. Let's keep this as our little secret."

He nodded vigorously and she noticed with satisfaction that he was sweating profusely throughout the rest of the dance. Once the set ended, he excused himself and hurried away. Lottie watched him closely as he pushed through the crowd, finally pausing to whisper frantically in Lady Hillington's ear.

Lady Hillington reddened at whatever news Sir Roland relayed and closed her fan with a snap. She shooed the large man away and looked around frantically.

"Only a few more to go," Lottie muttered to herself. She watched as the pair parted and hurried throughout the room to the other houseguests. Sir Roland spoke to Lord Campbell and Heather, while Lady Hillington found her son and clutched his arm.

Before she could gauge their reactions, a man stepped in front of her. She stifled a growl as she recognized Lord McCabe's cravat.

"Miss Lottie, please—"

"I will not marry you," Lottie snapped, drawing herself up to her full height—short as it was. "No matter what my brother-in-law has promised, I will never be your wife."

His head jerked back as if shocked by her fierce retort, and before he could stop her, she turned and disappeared into the crowd.

Her path was blocked once again by a tall man, but this time it was Mr. de Lacy. He took her hand and pulled her into the next set.

Lottie groaned, glancing over her shoulder in the direction of the laboratory. She had to get up there before the killer, or her plan would all be for naught.

"Looking for someone?" Mr. de Lacy asked, his voice pleasant even as his grip tightened around her.

She glared up at him. "The real killer."

He snorted with laughter. "Oh, little miss Lottie," he clucked his tongue. "You may have been able to hide the circumstances of my brother's death—for now—but you cannot ignore the evidence. I already arrested your stable hand, and it's only a matter of time before I find him—"

"I have it," Lottie interrupted.

Mr. de Lacy narrowed his eyes. "What?"

"What the real killer was looking for. Mr. Farraday's notebook."

His hands fell away and he stared at her. Before he could speak again, she spun on her heel and abandoned the dancefloor, mid-set.

Everyone knew now. She just had to get there in time.

The castle hallways were eerily dark, and her footsteps echoed as she ran. Her dress fluttered behind her as she took the stairs up to the tower two at a time, but she refused to slow.

The hinges creaked as she pushed the laboratory door open. "Sally?" she asked, peering around cautiously.

"Here, miss," Sally's small voice was muffled by the overturned table beside the door, but she was hidden well enough behind it that Lottie had not been able to see her in the darkness.

Panting, Lottie nodded. "Don't make a sound," she ordered, "no matter what happens, stick to the plan." Wintry moonlight spilled through the windows high above them, illuminating two patches in the center of the round room and Lottie kept an eye on the door as she quickly strapped the breastplate on and threw a cape around her shoulders.

The light glinting off the shiny metal blinked out as she closed the sides over her stomach. Thomas had fit it so well to her shape that even she wouldn't have been able to guess it was hidden beneath her long cape.

Breathing slowly to calm herself, Lottie stepped into the beam of moonlight, facing away from the door. This was it. All she needed now was the killer to take the bait.

She didn't have to wait long.

A few minutes passed before the door creaked behind her. Wishing desperately that she hadn't given her knife to Octavia, Lottie gripped the edges of the cape tighter over her stomach and remained still.

"Where is it?" a man growled behind her, his voice low and dangerous.

Lottie turned. "Lord Campbell."

*** Thomas grumbled under his breath as he searched the crowd for Lottie. He had been watching her the whole evening as men danced with her or tried to approach, but now he had lost her in the crowd.

"Stop fidgeting," William said, joining him at the edge of the room. "She's around here somewhere."

"Something feels wrong," Thomas clenched his fists. "We should have told her about our plan."

"Once the killer knows that you've escaped, he'll try to attack you again. Then we can catch him," William's tone was confident, but he, too, was beginning to search the room.

"What if Mr. de Lacy reveals it too soon?"

William shook his head. "You escaped from under his watch. It would be too embarrassing for him to reveal that. No, we shall bide our time until the right moment and reveal it ourselves."

Thomas swallowed hard. He would not be at ease until Lottie was safely at his side and the real killer caught.

*** "It was you?" Lottie blinked, wishing she had seen wrong. "B-but how?"

Lord Campbell smirked. "Yes, my 'idiot playboy' act is quite effective, isn't it?"

"You killed Mr. Farraday?" Lottie held her ground as he advanced. "Why?"

He shrugged, looking around at the room. Lottie had ordered the servants to move most of her inventions and some of the black powder and fireworks out to the parapets, fearing they could be damaged when she trapped the killer. Now, she was wishing she hadn't, for they could have provided her some barriers to hide behind.

"We were partners until he tried to cut me out," Lord Campbell strolled around her to the place where the spear had held the cogs of her giant clock in place. "I would seduce the young ladies and he would blackmail their families. It worked quite well, too. But then he just had to get greedy. He stopped sharing his evidence."

"The notebook," Lottie supplied, turning to face him. She needed to keep herself between him and the door.

Lord Campbell nodded. "Yes. But he grew suspicious. The notebook wasn't with him when I killed him. Wherever did you find it?"

"Did you move the body from the beach?" she asked, trying to redirect his attention.

"Very clever. Yes, I intended to frame you, but then that idiot, Thomas, had to be a hero and move the body to the beach. Once you left to find him, I took the body back and buried it behind the stables."

"And Mrs. Ashdown? Did you kill her, too?" Lottie lifted her chin in a show of bravery as he stepped closer until she could feel his hot breath on her cheeks.

"Nosy little thing, wasn't she?" he chuckled. "Yes. She saw me burying the body. Thankfully she wasn't able to tell that magistrate before I could poison her. She had the audacity to try blackmailing me, if you can believe it."

"But Catriona? How could you try to kill your own sister?" Lottie shook her head. His grief had seemed so genuine.

"Half-sister," Lord Campbell said, spitting on the ground as if the very mention of her defiled his tongue. "The little witch is hardly even human. It would have been nice if she'd drunk all the tea, but... alas. At least it allowed me to escape the magistrate's suspicion."

Rage burned Lottie's throat. "You're an animal."

He grabbed her by the neck of her cape, wrapping the fabric slowly around his fingers until she gasped for air. With methodical movements, he drew a long dagger and held it under her nose. Lottie swallowed hard, recognizing it from the forest. "Is your curiosity satisfied?" he growled. "Give me the notebook. Now."

"I don't have it," she choked back a cough and held his gaze, refusing to let him see her fear. The breastplate would protect her against the knife. "I lied." She smiled.

With a howl of fury, he plunged the dagger into her gut.

The tip of the blade pierced her armor. Her smile slipped and she gasped. Pain radiated from her stomach and up her spine as her lips parted in shock. Vaguely, she realized that the aged metal must have been weakened by reshaping.

With an animal-like snarl, Lord Campbell shoved the blade deeper.

An Explosive Ending

Lottie stumbled back as the knife dug into her. Her heel caught against her other ankle and she fell.

Lord Campbell released the knife, his gaze locked on hers as her shoulder blades collided with the hard floor.

Her ears rang and the room swam around her. In the distance, a woman screamed.

With a roar, the sound returned full force to her ears. Her head rolled to the side and she watched as Sally lurched to her feet from behind the table.

Lord Campbell hissed in annoyance and spun around.

He can't escape, Lottie clenched her jaw and snagged his ankle before he could give chase.

"Run!" she gasped, unable to draw a full breath.

Sally's hands clutched her hair as she screamed again and ran for the stairs.

"No!" Lord Campbell kicked backward into Lottie's chest, sending her sliding across the floor.

Gaping senselessly for air, she rolled onto her back, gazing up at the moonlight glinting off the handle of the dagger embedded in her gut. Had Sally made it down the stairs in time to lock the door at the bottom of the stairs before Lord Campbell escaped?

As her mind grew blurry from the blazing pain in her stomach, one thought prevailed. She had to lock the door to the castle parapets before Lord Campbell returned. That was the only way to trap him long enough for help to arrive.

Hands shaking, she gripped the handle. Even touching it sent waves of terror coursing through her. On instinct, she yanked. Metal screeched against metal as the knife pulled out of the breastplate and she dropped it beside her.

The ties to the breastplate loosened and it fell away as she rolled onto her side.

Warm blood met her fingers as she pressed her hand over the wound and forced herself to her feet. If she didn't get onto the parapets first, Lord Campbell would be back to finish her off.

The edges of her vision dimmed as she stumbled to the stairs. Leaning her shoulder against the spiral wall, her feet slipped against the stone steps. Pounding on the door at the bottom echoed up to her and she rested her head against the wall for a moment in relief.

Sally made it.

Falling forward, Lottie pressed on until at last, she reached the door leading out to the parapets. Footsteps thumped against the stairs below her. Lord Campbell was coming!

She fell against the door, pushing it out. With a cry, she slumped onto the rough stone, the bitterly cold wind biting her cheeks. She was running out of time.

Shoving herself up onto her knees, she used her shoulder to close the door behind her. One of the small barrels of black powder and several boxes of fireworks were stacked beside the door, shielding her somewhat from the wind. A small lantern swung above them, casting ominous shadows across the parapet.

Blood soaked the front of her dress and her hands shook as she reached for the key.

"Come... on..." she begged, stretching her fingers up until they brushed against the rusted metal key.

"Lottie!" Lord Campbell's voice raged behind the door.

Fear tightened Lottie's lungs and she whimpered, pressing her back against the door. Could she hold him off? "Heaven help me," she closed her eyes as he shoved against the wood, throwing her forward.

*** A woman's screams shattered the festive atmosphere of the ball and guests froze mid-dance.

Thomas grabbed William's arm and they both turned, searching for the source.

A maid ran into the ballroom, her face deathly pale as she sobbed. "Help! In the laboratory--With a knife--"

Thomas met the maid in the middle of the room, catching her when she tripped on her skirts. "Sally?" his stomach lurched when he recognized Lottie's maid. "What's happened?"

Sally shook her head, tears coursing down her cheeks. "He's killed her. Lord Campbell's killed Lottie!"

Thomas released her and ran, shoving guests aside in his haste.

William and Mr. de Lacy shouted after him, but he ignored them. Visions of Lottie lying lifeless clouded his mind. No, he forced them away. No, she can't be dead.

He slammed into the door at the bottom of the stairs leading up to the tower. The wood creaked but held.

"Lottie!" he shouted, throwing his shoulder against the door again and again. "Answer me, wee lassie!"

William and Fidelia arrived, panting, with Mr. de Lacy.

"Why won't it open?" William asked, slamming his hand against the door. In his panic, he had left his cane behind.

Mr. de Lacy examined the lock. "The key has been broken off inside."

"What are we going to do?" Fidelia cried.

"Is there another way to the castle parapets?" Thomas asked, looking around frantically.

"Across the courtyard," William pointed back the way they'd come. "But it will take too long—"

"Stay here and try to open the door," Thomas ordered. "I'll go."

I'm coming, Lottie, he thought as he ran through the darkened corridors. Hold on. Please hold on.

***

The door burst open, throwing Lottie forward. She landed hard and rolled, crying out as her wound twisted.

Lord Campbell emerged through the dark doorway, his normally well-kempt hair falling over his forehead as he panted, glowering at her. "Did you think you could outsmart me, you little wench?" he seethed.

Panic blinded her pain and Lottie clenched her fists, pushing herself to her feet. "It's... too late," she shook her head, her dancing shoes sliding across the stones as she backed away. "Everyone knows the truth now."

With a snarl, he tipped the small barrel of black powder over onto its side and kicked it toward her.

She threw herself to the side, landing against the wall that overlooked the courtyard. Her torso leaned dangerously over the edge.

*** Thomas burst into the castle's courtyard and skidded to a halt, gawking up at the wall.

A woman stood on the parapet. "Lottie!" he gasped, relief and horror warring within him.

She lunged to the side, halfway falling over the edge. "No!" Thomas screamed as she began to slip.

*** Lord Campbell's head jerked as someone shouted in the courtyard below.

Lottie scrabbled for a handhold, her nails digging in the stone wall. At last, she managed to pull herself upright and turned, gasping for air.

Lord Campbell yanked the swinging lantern from its place beside the door, marching closer.

Shaking her head desperately, Lottie pushed away from the wall and backed away toward the opposite side that looked out at the ocean.

"You just couldn't leave things alone, could you?" Lord Campbell growled, swinging the lantern at her. Lottie leaned away, the metal base of the lantern grazing the top of her head as it passed over her. "Why couldn't you just meekly give in like the other women?"

Her foot collided with the small barrel, and, in desperation, she shoved it toward him. He dodged it easily and it rolled back toward the boxes of fireworks, leaving a trail of black powder that seeped through a crack.

He swung the lantern again and she caught it before it could connect with her head, the hot metal and glass burning her hands.

She wrenched it from his grip, her back pressing into the wall. Frantically, she looked behind her. The net of her pulley system swung against the castle walls ten feet below... and tall, fluffy snowdrifts swam in her vision four stories down. Lord Campbell was too close for her to escape along the parapet.

She was trapped. But if he was going to send her to hades... she was taking him with her.

"I'm not like other women," Lottie whispered, slowly turning her gaze onto Lord Campbell.

"Then what are you?" he laughed, advancing until they were toe-to-toe.

"A killer," Lottie threw the lantern straight at his face.

He ducked just in time and the lit lantern sailed over his head, landing on the parapet hallway between them and the door.

Lord Campbell smirked. "You missed." He wrapped a large hand around her neck, cutting off her air.

She clawed at his fingers, her strength seeping away as he lifted her up until her feet kicked in empty air. Black spots burst in her vision, but she could hear the sizzling sound... and knew her desperate idea, her last hope... had succeeded.

"Didn't... miss..." she croaked, her lips twitching.

Lord Campbell's smile slipped, and he jerked his head around just as the flame from the shattered lantern traveled the final few feet to the barrel of black powder. His fingers released her neck.

*** The explosion rocked the castle, throwing Thomas to the ground.

His ears rang as he shook his head to clear it, looking up. Thick grey smoke roiled across the parapets, tendrils spinning over the wall and oozing down into the courtyard.

Fireworks shot into the air, bursting into bright stars high above the castle walls and illuminating ghostly patches of smoke where Lottie and Lord Campbell had been only moments ago.

"Lottie," Thomas breathed.

The crowd of guests that had flocked to the courtyard shouted and screamed in the confusion, but Thomas ignored them. Coughing in the thick smoke as fireworks continued to burst above him, he ran to the guard tower and took the stairs to the parapet two at a time.

He threw his shoulder against the door and fell onto the stone wall as the fireworks popped sporadically. Holding his arm over his nose to block out the smoke, he searched along the wall. "Lottie!" he coughed, waving his other hand through the cloud. "Lottie, where are ye?"

His steps slowed as a figure emerged through the darkness, leaning over the parapet. "Och, nay," he whispered, desperately praying he was wrong.

He grabbed the figure and hauled them back over the wall, gasping at the sight when he turned them over. The left side of Lord Campbell's face was covered in horrific burns, and blood trickled from his ears. Hands shaking, Thomas laid the man down on the ground and looked over the edge of the parapet, the heights making his vision waver.

"Lottie!" he screamed, his knees weakening when he finally spotted her.

Tangled in the netting of the pulley system, Lottie hung fifteen feet below. The ropes wrapped around her waist and chest holding her precariously as her head lolled to the side. Her feet swung in the air beneath her tattered dress.

"I'm coming, lassie, I'm coming," he repeated, leaning as far as he dared over the edge. The top connection to the pulley system had broken, all of her weight hanging by the remaining connection just above the top window.

He couldn't reach it!

"Wake up," he begged, leaning further. "Wake up, my love."

Slowly, her lashes fluttered. Her head remained unmoving as her lids lifted slightly.

"Oh, wee lassie," tears of relief pricked his eyes. "I can't reach ye from here," he shook his head, pulling himself back onto the wall. "I have to go down to the window. Don't move. Just stay still and hold on."

Her eyes drifted closed.

"Lottie?" his voice rose. Nothing. He slammed his fist against the stone and pushed away, searching for his way back to the guard tower. He had to get to the next floor down to reach her.

Every moment stretched into an eternity as he ran along the hallway, searching the windows for a glimpse of Lottie swinging from the netting.

At last, he spotted the rope through the glass. He yanked the window open just as the rope creaked. With a snap, the connection broke free of the wall.

"No!" Thomas lunged, snagging the end of the rope as it fell past the opening. The weight yanked him out and he shouted as he fell forward.

His other hand caught the lip of the window and they jerked to a stop. He cried out in pain as the sudden stop tore the stitches in his back. A few feet down, Lottie swung back and forth in the net.

Her lids opened again, and she gazed at him with unfocused eyes. "Thomas?" her voice broke and her hand reached weakly toward him.

"I've got ye," he assured, straining to maintain his grip on the rope. Hot blood trickled down his shoulder and arm from his reopened wounds, pooling between his fingers. The rope shifted slightly. "Keep yer eyes on me, wee lassie."

"I miss you," tears leaked from the corners of her eyes, tracing into the hair by her temples.

The rope slipped again, and she dropped a few inches.

Thomas shouted, desperately clutching at the rope. Muscles straining, he tried to lift her up, but the angle and his wounds combined to make it impossible. "Help!" he cried, looking over his shoulder as tears of hopelessness spilled onto his cheeks. "Please, someone, help her!"

"Should have told you..." Lottie's voice trailed off and Thomas looked down to see her eyes closing again.

"Stay awake," he begged as the blood soaked into the rope, droplets falling from his knuckles and splattering onto her cheeks.

"I love you," she whispered.

Blood slipped between his fingers and the fibers, and the rope slid from his grasp.

"No!" Thomas screamed, watching helplessly.

Lottie fell the remaining two stories, the grey cloud enveloping her. The thump echoed through the night.

Love At Last

Thomas found Lottie half-submerged in the fluffy snowdrifts at the base of the castle wall. Her pale hair, now stained with blood, fanned around her like a dark halo. Hands shaking, he touched her cold cheek. Her breath warmed his hand.

She was still alive.

He gathered her into his arms, cradling her face. "Lassie?" he whispered, pressing a soft kiss to her forehead. "Please don't go." His voice broke and he glanced down, his heart thudding at the sight of the dark blood staining the snow.

He pressed his hand over the wound in her stomach and buried his face against her neck, hot tears burning his eyes. "Please stay with me."

*** Two days later, Thomas sat at Lottie's bedside, holding her hand as his head tipped forward in exhaustion.

"You should rest," William said quietly, nudging Thomas awake.

He jerked upright, sighing and rubbing his eyes when he realized it was just his old friend. "I don't want to leave her," he watched as her check rose and fell slowly.

Thankfully, the snow had cushioned her fall and she only sustained a broken wrist and bruised ribs. The stab wound in her stomach had been frightful, but the doctor said it wasn't deep enough to do serious damage. He had been able to stitch it closed... but Lottie still hadn't awakened.

"How is Lord Campbell?" Thomas asked, changing the subject as he readjusted the blankets closer to Lottie's chin.

William sat in one of the other chairs and cringed, massaging his old wound. "The burns from the blast were quite serious. He's lucky to have survived at all. Still, he has yet to regain his hearing."

Thomas nodded and brushed his thumb along Lottie's cheek. The tips of her hair had singed, but she was otherwise unharmed by the blast. They suspected that Lord Campbell had dropped her over the edge of the parapet wall just before the explosion, inadvertently protecting her. "If only Lottie hadn't gone so far to reveal the truth," he said, staring at her peaceful face.

William sighed and patted Thomas on the shoulder. "Get some rest. I'll go check on Fidelia. The doctor fears that the shock has caused some distress for the pregnancy."

After the door closed behind him, Thomas climbed hesitantly onto the bed beside Lottie and laid his head beside hers on the pillow, pressing his lips to her shoulder in a gentle kiss. He curled his body as close as he dared to hers, careful of her many injuries, and closed his eyes. "Come back to me."

*** Lottie was falling. Falling, watching a sky full of fire above her... and Thomas's hand reaching out. Over and over, she felt the tattered remains of her dress flutter around her as she fell, weightless, to the ground. Each time, she braced for the impact, dreading the pain, utter terror enveloping her mind.

Is this how Le Coquin felt? She wondered as she fell endlessly. Is this my punishment?

"Come back to me," a familiar voice whispered in her ear. Warmth spread across her shoulder and neck as someone breathed beside her, pulling her out of her terror.

Thomas? She tried to call out to him, but her lips wouldn't move.

The dream continued, but this time she fell without fear, looking around for her Scotsman.

"Thomas?" William's voice pierced the shadowy dream. "Someone's here to see you. I think you'd better go."

The warmth beside her vanished.

No, she reached for him. Slowly, her eyes opened, and she looked up at the canopy over her bed, safe in the familiarity of her own bedroom.

"Lottie?" William and Fidelia gasped simultaneously from somewhere nearby.

She groaned as she turned her head. Her neck ached terribly. William grasped her hand and Fidelia wrapped her arms around her, crying.

"Send for the earl and countess," William ordered a servant.

"Where's Thomas?" Lottie asked, her voice hoarse.

*** Thomas stared at the imposing man who stood before the fire in the library, his back to him. "Father."

The Duke of Argyle turned and nodded stiffly. "Thomas. It's... been far too long."

"What do ye want?" Thomas asked, ignoring the attempt at a greeting. His father had made it quite clear two years ago that he wished his son had died in the war.

The duke coughed into his fist and straightened. "Your brother has caused quite a stir, so I'm told."

"He's killed two people," Thomas snapped. "Not to mention poisoning my sister and stabbing the woman I love."

The duke ground his teeth. His eldest son had always been his favorite, and Thomas knew that the children from his second marriage were simple afterthoughts to him. "Yes, well." the duke clasped his hands behind his back and turned back to the fire. "For these crimes, he shall be stripped of his title. Thus... I find myself in need of an heir to the Campbell clan and to the duchy. You shall return to Scotland immediately and prepare to take his position."

Thomas clenched his hands into fists. After all this time, his father had the audacity to demand that he return and take up his foolish brother's position? "No." He turned and yanked the door open.

"If you want to provide any sort of life for that young lady, then you will reconsider your response," the duke said, his voice dark with warning.

Thomas paused, dread filling his gut. His father was right. He needed to be responsible for her... and he couldn't do that if he spent the rest of his life hiding who he really was. She deserved more than a stable hand damaged by the war. "Let me say goodbye."

*** Thomas slowed as he neared Lottie's room when he heard the happy voices inside. He held his breath. Did that mean...? Hesitantly, he opened the door a crack and peered in.

Lottie's family gathered around her, smiling and crying. She sat upright in the bed, propped up by several pillows, grinning weakly at them.

Thomas sighed in relief and rested his head against the wall, watching her. It was like seeing her wake from the dead after so many days of worrying, praying, and hoping. Could she accept him if she knew the truth? Would knowing his relation to Lord Campbell be too much for her? His heart fell as he gazed at her through the crack.

Lottie turned toward the door, her eyes hopeful. His gut tightened and he closed the door before she could spot him. Was he, a man who had run from his duty and identity, even worthy of her?

*** Three months later, Lottie gazed out the window as the carriage jostled her. She sighed, numb to the beautiful wintry landscape that passed by. She had never been to Scotland before, but it was hard to muster any excitement.

"Try to smile, dear," the countess patted her hand, sharing a secretive smile with Fidelia. "You are about to meet your fiancé, after all."

Lottie withheld another sigh and nodded. The past months of her recovery had been overshadowed by the fact that no one would speak about Thomas. Had she imagined that he had been there when she fell from the parapet? Surely, he would have come to see her if he had been released from prison by Mr. de Lacy?

After a week of pestering, she had finally given in to her family's demand that she travel to Scotland to meet Lord McCabe. But her heart felt heavy and numb.

The tall, grey walls of Inveraray Castle rose in the distance, four turrets disappearing in the snowy fog. Once they arrived, it seemed that the entirety of the castle servants had turned out to greet their new mistress, and even the duke of argyle offered a begrudging "how do you do, Miss Lottie."

"Lottie!" Catriona cried happily, throwing her arms around the other woman.

"It's good to see you," Lottie replied in earnest. "You seem to have recovered well?"

Catriona nodded and gave a little twirl. "As have you. I was so worried when I heard what happened."

Lottie forced a smile, but it was pained. She didn't like to relive the memories of that night. "Where is my betrothed?"

Catriona's grin turned mischievous. "Oh, he's around here somewhere. Why don't you explore the castle a little before supper? I think you'll find the East Tower to be particularly interesting."

Lottie's family quickly abandoned her and she found herself wandering the ancient castle halls alone. Her curiosity finally getting the best of her, she climbed the spiral stairs to the East Tower and gasped at the top.

Long tables crossed the round room, new equipment and instruments set atop. Tall windows lined the walls, flooding the space with natural light, while a warm fire crackled to her left.

"Puppy?" she exclaimed, shocked to see her beloved cat curled on a plush armchair near the fire. Had William sent him along ahead of her?

The cat purred in greeting and stretched languidly, clawing at the velvet.

She left him to his slumber and examined the room, pausing by a tripod set up beside one of the windows. She clasped her hands together. She had never seen a telescope in person before.

"Do ye like it?" a warm voice spoke just behind her.

Lottie gasped, spinning to face the intruder. "Thomas?"

Her handsome Scotsman stood before her, his dark, curly hair freshly cut and styled in the latest fashion, and his broad shoulders accentuated by an expensive suitcoat. He smiled broadly, reaching up to cup her cheek. "Hello, wee lassie."

Lottie pulled back, shaking her head. "But... I-I don't understand. What are you doing here?"

His smile faded. "I suppose I should introduce myself properly," he sketched a graceful bow. "Lord Thomas McCabe, the second son of the Duke of Argyle... and his heir."

Lottie stared at him, praying this wasn't a dream. "You... lied to me?"

He nodded guiltily. "Lord Campbell is my half brother, and Catriona is my sister. She was just a child when I left. Hawthorne is my mother's maiden name. The McCabe title is passed from her father's line. After I returned from the war... I didn't want to be Lord McCabe anymore. I didn't even want to live. I just... existed. Until I met ye."

She stared at him for a long moment and turned to the window, biting her thumbnail as her mind raced. So it had all been a trick? William and Fidelia had kept the truth from her, even though they knew how much it hurt her that they had engaged her to Lord McCabe? And Thomas had played along?

"Are ye mad?" Thomas asked.

Lottie scoffed. "Of course I am! Do you have any idea how much I feared you were-" she broke off and choked back a sob.

Warm arms wrapped around her from behind, holding her gently. Thomas bent and rested his chin on her shoulder. "Forgive me, wee lassie. We feared what the ton would say about ye if anyone knew that Thomas Hawthorne had survived. It would be quite the scandal if ye married a stable hand...

and I did nay feel worthy of ye as I was. I had to accept my responsibility. I had to be a man ye could be proud of... someone who took care of his people, not ran away from it all."

Lottie closed her eyes and turned in his embrace, burying her head against his chest. "I missed you," she whispered. "I was so worried about you."

He held her tightly, pressing his cheek against her hair. "I'll nay leave ye again for the rest of my life," he promised.

She wrapped her hands around the back of his neck and pulled him toward her, rising onto her toes to meet his lips.

Thomas's sound of surprise was cut off as she kissed him, threading her fingers into his curly hair.

With a happy growl, he returned her kiss with equal fervor.

Breathless, they broke apart.

"I love you," she said, her heart pounding with joy as she clutched his lapels. At last, she had claimed Thomas forever and always.

Thomas laughed and lifted her feet from the ground, spinning her around as he shouted, "I love ye, I love ye!" Lottie threw her head back and giggled.

At last, all was right with the world.

Epilogue

27th July 1814, Lampton Castle

Lottie grinned at the bright green eyes of the tiny baby girl that stared up at her. "Oh, she's perfection," she whispered, nudging Thomas.

"Och, watch it," Thomas yelped. "Ye'll make me drop him," he pulled away, frantically patting the back of the blue-eyed baby boy in his arms.

Lottie giggled and nudged him again. "You don't have to pat him so much. Just bounce him gently, like this," she demonstrated, carefully bouncing her swaddled bundle.

The newlyweds of five months had traveled to Lampton Castle just in time for Fidelia's labor, which lasted nearly fifteen hours. To their great surprise and delight, they finally learned the reason for her severe pregnancy symptoms: twins.

William opened the door to their bedroom and smiled in spite of the dark circles beneath his eyes. "She's awake," he said, holding a finger to his lips and gesturing for them to come in.

Fidelia lay in the bed, her coppery curls plastered to her forehead and neck with sweat. She held her arms out and Lottie placed the bundle into the new mother's hands.

"Oh," Fidelia's eyes brimmed with tears. "My sweet Aurelia," she pressed her lips to the baby's nose and was rewarded with a screech of annoyance from the tiny girl. Fidelia smiled and snuggled her cheek against the baby's dark brown hair.

"She has your temper," William teased. He took the baby boy from Thomas and placed him beside his sister. "Now, our handsome Philip has my good disposition," he said proudly, brushing the boy's red hair back from his forehead.

William kissed his wife tenderly and sat beside her on the bed so she could lean against him for support. The labor had left her quite exhausted, it seemed.

The earl and countess joined them and together, they admired the new additions to the family, trying to pinpoint which features resembled which relative amid much laughter.

Thomas wrapped his arms around Lottie's waist, one hand resting against her stomach lightly. "We shall have to work hard to catch up," he whispered in her ear teasingly.

Lottie giggled and flicked his nose lightly, "Oh, hush."

She leaned her head back against her husband's chest, relishing the warmth of his embrace as she gazed at her beloved family. They had all fought through so much for so long to be here.

She was no longer haunted by the memories of Le Coquin and Edmund, having finally accepted that she was not responsible for their selfish actions, nor had she sinned against God for protecting herself.

Although she could still feel phantom pain in her stomach, the wound had healed to a dark scare, and she jumped a little less each time a loud noise startled her. With Thomas's gentle, constant love, her heart was healing.

A servant knocked on the door and delivered a letter to William, whose face darkened when he saw the handwriting.

He kissed Fidelia on the forehead and stepped away to read the letter in the light of the window. He gawked, blinking rapidly. "How is this possible?"

"What is it?" Lottie asked, unease causing the hairs along her arms to raise.

William shook his head and held up the letter. "I received a message from one of my spies in America."

"Is it news of Charles?" Fidelia asked eagerly, sitting upright. Aurelia cooed and Philip stretched his tiny arms above his head.

William hesitated. Finally, he grimaced. "My spy says he saw Miss Octavia Palmer near new Orleans. She has been taken captive by pirates and the captain has claimed her as his woman..." Wiliam cleared his throat and read the final words from the letter. "The pirate captain Charles Atwell."

The End

**